HERE I AM

HERE I AM

*Exploring Christ's Thoughts, Feelings, And
Relationship With God The Father*

JULIA BALDWIN

XULON PRESS

Xulon Press
2301 Lucien Way #415
Maitland, FL 32751
407.339.4217
www.xulonpress.com

Unless otherwise indicated, Scripture quotations taken from the Holy Bible, New International Version (NIV). Copyright © 1973, 1978, 1984, 2011 by Biblica, Inc.™. Used by permission. All rights reserved.

Scripture quotations taken from the English Standard Version (ESV). Copyright © 2001 by Crossway, a publishing ministry of Good News Publishers. Used by permission. All rights reserved.

Scripture quotations taken from the American King James Version (AKJV)–*public domain.*

Scripture quotations taken from the Holy Bible, New Living Translation (NLT). Copyright ©1996, 2004, 2007 by Tyndale House Foundation. Used by permission of Tyndale House Publishers, Inc.

Printed in the United States of America.

ISBN-13: 978-1-54565-288-6

PREFACE

—◈—

"Have you ever considered writing a book?" This was a question I would be asked every time I told someone I was an English major. My initial answer would be, "No. At least, not for the foreseeable future."

If it was a family member or a friend who knew me well, they would half-jokingly follow their question with, "Knowing you, you'd probably write a book about Jesus, huh?" At this, I would just smile and shrug my shoulders. The truth was that I had gone into English with the hopes of one day becoming an English teacher, or perhaps even a professor. I liked writing, knew I was gifted in the art, and even had my own personal blog. However, the thought of writing an actual book for hundreds of thousands of people to read just seemed sort of scary to me.

That is until one of my writing professors gave my class a short writing assignment right before Christmas break, asking us to write a piece of prose poetry about one aspect of the Christmas season. I instantly thought of the Nativity and decided to write a short piece from the Christ Child's perspective. That Christmas, I placed my poem on the family room table for my guests to read when they came for Christmas dinner, and they were all very impressed.

Fast-forward to second and final semester, when I was anxiously preparing to write my senior thesis and brainstorming what I was going to write it on. My mind wandered back to two events: first, the time I wrote my Nativity poem, and second, my amazing Juniors Abroad trip. I had chosen to go on the Israel-Jordan route. Having learned a lot about life and the culture in the Holy Lands *and* written a poem about the beginning of Jesus' earthly life, I thought, "I've just got to do more with this!" That is how *Here I Am: Exploring Christ's Thoughts, Feelings, and Relationship with God the Father* came to be.

A word of warning: This book is not like any other book about the life of Christ that you might have read. For one thing, it *is* narrated by Jesus Christ Himself. Therefore, there is more detail throughout the chapters and events of His life than the actual gospels, or even another book of the same subject, might give. This is simply to make Jesus feel more real, more relatable, and maybe even more dynamic to the reader and not to suggest any personal theological beliefs.

Another thing that makes this book different from others is that God the Father is a more present and prominent Figure in the book and in Jesus' life. As Jesus, so often in His ministry, went off on His own to pray, it only seemed right to imagine what He would have talked to His Father about and how His Father would answer. I wanted to portray God not just as a *Father* (biological) but as a *Dad* (relational) to Jesus, still taking the redemption plan into account but also portraying the love, warmth, sorrow, and even playfulness shared between the duo, like a natural father-son relationship (think Mufasa and Simba from *The Lion King*).

Lastly, there is a slightly larger emphasis put on Jesus' human nature than His divine nature, though for the most part, I do try to balance the two. Don't get me wrong, I have still recorded many of the miracles and times when Jesus demonstrates His authority, to be sure. However, I focus mostly on His love, compassion, friendship, and emotional side. There are even some parts where He doubts Himself and needs encouragement and guidance from His Father. The reason I write Him in this way is two-fold: Firstly, I wanted Him to be seen as an example, learning and growing alongside the reader in His walk with the Father, and thus teaching humility and dependence on God. Secondly, I wanted to portray the love God has for the reader through His love for His Son in how He speaks to Him and, in turn, how Christ speaks to His disciples.

The book's target audience is those who want to know Jesus not just as a historical figure, but also as a real person intimately connected to His Father and with a passion for humankind. I do not want my readers to feel as though they are simply watching a movie *about* Jesus' life; rather, I want them to feel as though they are *there,* walking alongside Jesus, hearing His voice, seeing His tears, and sharing His joys.

Whether you are new to the Christian faith or have been a Christian for many years, I pray that you fall in love with your Lord and Savior, Jesus Christ, as never before while He takes you by the hand and draws you into His world through *Here I Am: Exploring Christ's Thoughts, Feelings, and Relationship with God the Father.*

God bless all,

J. B.

In the beginning was the Word,

and the Word was with God and the Word was God. He

was with God in the beginning. Through Him, all things

were made; without Him, nothing was made that has

been made. In Him was life, and that life was the light

of all mankind. The light shines in the darkness, and the

darkness has not overcome it. The Word became flesh

and made His dwelling among us. We have seen His

glory, the glory of the one and only Son, who came from

the Father, full of grace and truth.

John 1:1–5; 14

CHAPTER 1

"Why were you searching for Me?
Didn't you know I had to be in My Father's house?"
—Jesus (Luke 2:49)

———◈◈◈———

T he Mediterranean morning sunlight streaks through my bedroom window and into my slowly opening eyes. I sit up in bed, yawning and stretching, when it occurs to me: *Passover week! It begins today!* Since my twelfth birthday, I have been eagerly awaiting this week of traveling, worshiping, and feasting with my parents. I spring out of bed and sprint out to wake my parents, ignoring the pain in my toe after I stub it on my bedroom door.

"Mama! Papa! Wake up!" I call. "We're going to Jerusalem!"

My parents clothe themselves and emerge from their room. They are groggy, yet happy and ready for the long trek ahead.

———◈◈◈———

Like a deer through a field of wildflowers, my feet barely touch the ground as I skip along the road leading to Jerusalem

1

and King Solomon's glorious temple. I only stop to help Mama and Papa lift our cart when it hits a stone. Finally, after what seems like forever and a day, I see the temple in the distance, gleaming in the sun as if radiating the glory of God Himself.

Mama stays behind in the women's court while Papa and I select a lamb to give to the high priest as a sacrifice. As Papa takes a lamb and places it in my arms to carry up the steps, a new sensation washes over me. For the first time, I feel a sense of sorrow concerning the practice of sacrifice. I have been taught that people take innocent, spotless, young animals and burn them so as to let the wrath of God come down on the animals so that sinful, imperfect people may be free from that wrath. However, as I feel this innocent, spotless, frightened lamb struggle in my arms and listen to its bleats and cries for its mother, my eyes fill with tears. Tears for the people oppressed and burdened by their sin and shame; tears for these perfect, helpless animals who have done no wrong to deserve such punishment. As I approach the high priest to give him my sacrifice, he notices my grave, disconsolate expression and says, "Be of good cheer, son. The Passover feast begins!"

The days fly by like swallows. I learn more about the Lord and about His word; days of eating delicious food, including lamb meat, which I almost never get to eat at home, and I worship with my parents and friends I have made during our pilgrimage. Before I know it, my mother takes my hand and says, "Son, it's time to go home now." I am a little sad that my highly anticipated week is ending, but I obediently begin walking in my parents' direction back to our humble town of Nazareth.

Suddenly, I feel a hand lightly plant itself onto my shoulder. Alarmed, I quickly turn to see if someone in the crowd has bumped against me by mistake. No one shows his or herself or offers a plea for pardon, but I still feel the presence of the hand on my shoulder. Soon, a voice begins to speak:

"Stay here with Me a little while longer, My Son."

A thrill shoots up my spine like a bolt of lightning. *Stay here a little while longer? This place where I feel more at home than in my own hometown at times? This invitation seems too good to be true! Is it?*

In spite of myself, I whisper, "Really? Can I?"

But then I think of my parents. *How worried and sad they would be to find that I had left them.*

"Oh, but what about Mama and Papa? They are sure to worry and miss me very much."

"Fear not, My Son. I will only keep You here for three more days. And yes, Your parents will indeed worry and miss You greatly. However, they need not worry, for I will be with You and protect You and will bring You back to Your parents when the time comes. I am keeping You in this place to strengthen You and prepare You for Your future. You are too young to fully grasp these future plans, but I have instilled in You a vast knowledge of Me to share with My servants. Go. Head back towards the temple courts and I will introduce You to them."

—◈—

Eagerly, I walk up the steps to the men's court of the temple. Upon approaching closer, I soon hear the garbled, sober voices of the teachers of the law. In front of them is the first scroll of the Torah:

"Then Abraham reached out his hand and took the knife to slaughter his son. But the angel of the Lord called to him from heaven and said, 'Abraham, Abraham-'

"Do not lay your hand on the boy or do anything to him, for now I know that you fear God, seeing you have not withheld your son, your only son, from Me [1]."

These words flow right out of my mouth before I can stop them. Feeling all eyes on me, I hang my head in shame.

"Forgive me, Sirs. I have spoken out of turn."

I lift my head and see that the teachers of the law are still staring at me. In their eyes are expressions of awe and surprise.

"How do you remember that exact line of text in its entirety, young man?"

I hesitate before answering, "To be honest, I don't know; the words just came out."

"How old are you?" asks the rabbi.

"Twelve years old, Sir," I answer. "This week was my first Passover, and—"

"And you had such a great time, you don't want to leave? Is that it, Boy?" one of the other teachers says with a chuckle. "Aren't your parents around?"

"Well … er …" I am not prepared to answer this question.

---

[1] Genesis 22:12

"Well, never mind," the rabbi walks up to me and claps me gently on the back. "After all, it is written in the scriptures, 'Better is one day in Your courts than a thousand elsewhere.'"

"Is that Psalm 84, line ten?" I surmise.

"Why yes, it is!" the rabbi exclaims in great astonishment. "How do you know so much for such a young boy? God must surely have blessed you with the knowledge of Himself and His word, has He not?"

*God? It was God who spoke to me earlier? It must have been! But that means **I'm** the Son of God? **I'm** the promised Messiah I've grown up hearing about? Could it be true?*

"Excuse me, Sirs, but were you in the middle of studying the story of Father Abraham and Isaac?"

"Yes, we were, and we could use one more scholar in our midst!"

"Sure, I'd love to join!"

The rabbi takes me by the hand and leads me into the circle of teachers and scholars of the law. I feel a little shy but very excited to be invited into a bazaar.

"What is your name, son?"

"Jesus. Jesus Bar-Joseph,[2] Sir."

---

[2] In the Hebrew language, the surname "Bar-" is used in the place of a last name, meaning "Son of-"

"Well, Jesus, you seem to know the story of Father Abraham and Isaac quite well already. Do you have any questions concerning it?"

"Well, Sir, one question I have is, how old would you say Isaac was when Father Abraham was told to sacrifice him?"

One of the teachers speaks up now and says, "Well, scripture never gives us an exact age. But if I had to venture an estimate, I would say that he would have been between the ages of ten and twelve, around your age, perhaps younger. The reason why is that that age marks the cutoff point of a child's innocence. Isaac would have had to be innocent to be used for a sacrifice."

"Sir, why would God ask Father Abraham to sacrifice his own son instead of the usual lamb?"

"Well, He wanted to see if Father Abraham loved and trusted Him enough to sacrifice the one thing most precious to him."

"Yes, but God knows all things, doesn't He? Wouldn't He already know that Father Abraham would do it?"

Here, the whole council of teachers and scholars goes silent. It seems that no one was expecting the question I asked. I can feel my face turning red. Have I said something wrong? To spare me further embarrassment, one of the teachers breaks the silence, "Well, son, that is a very good question you have proposed. I am afraid we do not have a concrete answer to this. Would *you* have any ideas as to why He would?"

Again, I am at a loss for words. Finally, one of the older scholars speaks up:

"I do not know the exact reason, other than in the third scroll of Moses,[3] God made a law forbidding child sacrifice. Therefore, it is probable that He never wanted Father Abraham to actually sacrifice his son. Also, God repeated His promise to Father Abraham that He would bless him with many descendants after Isaac. Perhaps the test was merely a setup to this blessing. I would not worry about this matter, son. The point is that Isaac was spared and lived for 180 years. Isn't that so?"

"Yes Sir, I suppose that's true," I say, although still not completely satisfied. My mind wanders back to the beginning of this week, when I had the lamb in my arms and I was weeping over it. The thought of killing a young animal, even if it was for God, felt terrible enough. I can scarcely imagine sacrificing a human child, around the same age as myself.

—⟨∞⟩—

Today marks the third morning of my stay in Jerusalem. It has been amazing: Yesterday, we went through the prophets,

---

[3] See Leviticus 20:2–5

beginning with Moses. We discussed the reason for the Passover and God's presence and provision for His people, the Israelites, through the wilderness. Now, we are studying the scroll of Isaiah:

"And the virgin shall conceive and give birth to a son, and they shall call him Immanuel, which means, 'God with us.'"[4]

"Sir?"

"Yes, Son?"

"Who is Isaiah referring to in this passage?"

"Well, many of us interpret this to mean there was a woman that Isaiah knew who was pregnant at the time. Isaiah is prophesying that the child's birth would mark the end of the Babylonian exile and God's return to His people, Israel."

"Well, Sir, that is certainly a valid interpretation. However, is that the *only* way one could read it?"

"Well, what do *you* suggest it means, my boy?"

"Well, couldn't it also be symbolic of the coming Messiah, the Son of God? The passage says that the pregnant woman would be a *virgin,* doesn't it? The only way a woman could be pregnant without knowing a man would be by divine intervention, a miraculous encounter with God."

---

[4] Isaiah 7:14

What I dare not tell them is that my very own mother was a—

"Jesus Bar-Joseph! There you are!"

My train of thought is broken by the desperate cries of Mama and the frantic footsteps of both my parents as they sprint up the steps and Papa takes me firmly by the arm.

"My apologies, Rabbi, for any trouble my son may have caused."

The rabbi laughs and says, "Trouble? Your boy is an excellent scholar! He has been with us these past two days, just listening to our teachings, asking the most profound questions, and sometimes offering even more profound answers to ours! I tell you, he will grow up to be a wondrous young man one of these days! We were just talking over the Messianic prophecies found in the scroll of Isaiah—"

"Well, I think that is plenty for a young boy in one day," Mama chimes in curtly. "Good-bye and thank you for watching our son."

Once we reach the bottom step, Mama stops and demands, "My son, why have you done this to us? Your father and I have been searching anxiously for you for three days now! We couldn't sleep; we couldn't eat; we couldn't do anything but worry and pray and search for you! What do you have to say for yourself?"

I listen patiently to Mama's scolding. Once she finishes, I gently take her face in my hands so that our eyes are on the same level and say in a gentle voice, "Mama, why were you worried? Why did you have to look for Me?[5] Surely you must have known I would be in My Father's house."

Mama's expression softens like wax, but her eyes go wide and round as tombstones. She shoots Papa a glance that I translate to mean, *"He knows?"* As if reading her thoughts, Papa shrugs and nods, a bit of a sad expression in his eyes. After a moment, he clears his throat and murmurs, "Son, please just come home with us for now. We know that Your true Father has great plans for You and will use You in a mighty way for His glory. But You still have some growing up to do before then, and we want You, for just a little while longer, to simply be *our* child. Won't You come home?"

With a sad smile, I nod and say, "Yes, Papa. I will."

Upon hearing this, My parents smile and sigh in tired relief, take Me by both arms, and together we make the journey home to our little village in Nazareth. As we are walking, I hear the gentle voice of God My Father say, "Let it be so, My Son. Go home with Your parents and obey them. I will be with You and

---

[5] From this point onward, Jesus' personal pronouns will be capitalized to indicate His acknowledgment of His divine identity.

will bring You back to this place when it is time. You will grow in stature and wisdom. Those whom You encounter will look on You with favor. And so will I[6]."

---

[6] See Luke 2:52

CHAPTER 2
Eighteen Years Later

"Look! The Lamb of God who takes away the sin of the world!"
—John the Baptist (John 1:29)

"Let it be so now; it is proper for us to do this to fulfill all righteousness."
—Jesus to John the Baptist (Matthew 3:15)

———

My day would not be complete without hearing his far-off clarion call from the bank of the Jordan River. Sometimes his voice was an exuberant, elated song of "Prepare ye the way of the Lord," and sometimes it would take on the tone of a displeased, righteously angry judge hissing, "You brood of vipers! Who warned you to flee the coming day of God's wrath?" This is the voice of a man I know and love very much. This is the voice of My dear cousin,[7] John Bar-Zechariah.

———

It is a fascinating story of how his parents found out about him. It was My uncle Zechariah's turn to offer the incense in

---

[7] They were actually second cousins. Their mothers were first cousins.

the temple. As he was offering it, one of My very own angels, Gabriel, appeared to him and announced that Aunt Elizabeth would become pregnant and give birth to John, the forerunner of the Messiah. He would be the one to help turn the people's hearts back to God and prepare for the Messiah's coming.

Of course, like the patriarch Abraham before him, My uncle scoffed at this news, as he and his wife were already advanced in their years, and like Sarah, My aunt was barren. As a result of his disbelief, Gabriel took away Zechariah's speech for nine months.[8]

When Elizabeth was six months pregnant with John, My mother came to visit. As soon as the sound of My mother's greeting rang in Elizabeth's ears, John's spirit acknowledged My presence. How he recognized Me at only six months is a mystery, but he was so excited and filled with joy that he leaped inside his mother's womb![9] John and I always laugh at this part of the story whenever either of our mothers retells it to us.

The day John was circumcised, everyone in his household wanted him to be named Zachariah, after his father. However, Elizabeth said that his name must be John, in accordance with

---

[8] See Luke 1:5–20

[9] See Luke 1:39–45

Gabriel's instructions. At first, they objected, as no one in their family was named John. They turned to Zachariah to ask him what he wanted his son to be named. As My uncle still could not speak, he etched out the words on a slate, "His name is John." Once John's name was spelled out, My uncle's tongue was loosened, and he could speak again.[10]

—⁓⁓—

In recent years, John has traded his leaping legs for a mighty voice that would put any priest's shofar[11] to shame. This voice, along with his excitement and fiery passion, makes My coming and presence known to everyone who will listen. I can tell that he is quite a convincing preacher. Just this morning, some tax collectors and Roman centurions had come asking how to live a more righteous life. To the tax collectors, My cousin instructed, "Don't collect any more than you are required to." To the Roman centurions, he commanded, "Be content with your pay. Do not exhort money or accuse people falsely."

Anticipation and joy fill My heart as I approach the Jordan, where John is waiting for new people to preach to and baptize.

---

[10] See Luke 1:57–64

[11] Ram's horn blown by the priests in the Temple

It has been years since I have last seen him. I wonder if he will remember Me as his cousin and not just as the Messiah.

By this time, My cousin's voice has gone raspy and hoarse, strained from calling and shouting out to the crowd all week, no doubt. My hand taps his camel-hair-covered shoulder a couple times. These shoulders, when John was but a springy, nimble young boy with curly hair, were once dotted with freckles. Now, the number of freckles has decreased by at least half, and in their place are scars from honeybee stings John has suffered in his pursuit of their succulent, golden treasure.

When John turns around and find himself face-to-face with Me, his stony, tenacious expression softens. The fight that he had inside of him earlier loosens up and a demeanor of humility and meekness overtakes him. In a voice that's dying yet somehow loud enough to be heard by much of the crowd, he utters, "Look! The Lamb of God who takes away the sin of the world!"

After these words have left his lips, John breaks into a smile, turns, and throws his arms around Me. "Cousin! Cousin Jesus," he exclaims. "How I've missed You these past years! Tell me, do You remember me at all?"

My heart nearly explodes with joy as I hug him back and tell him, "Of course I do, cousin! I remember all the games we used to play down here along this bank. We would skip stones and splash each other as we swam in the river. Some days, we would even fight using the reeds as swords! Yes, I remember it all!"

"Want to have a reed battle right now? Just for old time's sake?" John asks, winking at Me to signal that he is joking.

"No thank you, John," I say with a small laugh. "Actually, I have come to get washed up, and I need *you* to wash Me."

The smile falls from My cousin's face as he processes My words and what they mean. He is barely able to maintain eye contact as he stammers, "W-what? *You* come to *me?* Jesus, You've got it wrong. *I'm* the one who needs to be baptized by *You.* I am not even fit to carry Your sandals, let alone wash You as I would any sinful man."

My heart melts from My cousin's humility, and I stroke his neck in a reassuring manner. "No, no. Please John, let it be this way now. We need to do all that God requires us to. This task is given us to fulfill all righteousness."

John hesitates for only a moment longer before nodding and saying, "Yes, You're right. If this is God's will for me to baptize You, I will obey."

He leads Me deeper into the river and pushes My head under the water. Only a couple moments pass until I feel a warm and electrifying sensation. It is the same sensation I felt eighteen years ago in the temple when I first heard the voice of My true Father speak to Me. Eagerly, I push back up to the surface. To My amazement, the whole riverbank is bathed in light, and the single patch of clouds has rolled back like a scroll.

The sun's light intensifies by seven-fold at least, and I hear a familiar voice from heaven ringing out, "You are My beloved Son! I delight in You! Everyone, look at My beloved Son! I am well pleased with Him!"

As the last word echoes in My ear, a small piece of white comes fluttering down from the break in the clouds. Upon descending closer, it takes on the shape of a dove, and I soon hear it cooing. It lands on My shoulder and affectionately nuzzles up against My neck. I realize now that this is not an *it*; rather, this is a *He*. He is the Holy Spirit, the person My Father has sent to guide Me and protect Me throughout My future endeavors.

—◦◦◦—

I hug John and turn to leave. My cousin calls to Me, "Wait! Jesus, are You leaving so soon? You just got here."

I smile sadly at him and call back, "I am sorry, Cousin. I must follow wherever the Spirit leads from now on. I will miss you, but this is for the best."

John lowers his eyes and nods. "Yes, I understand. God be with You, Cousin."

"And with you," I say. With that, I continue on My way to the wilderness. My heart is heavy with the thought that I might never see My beloved cousin again. However, I know that I must do whatever God's will is for Me during these next few years.

Chapter 3

"Get behind Me, Satan! For it is written:
'Worship the Lord your God, and serve Him alone.'"
—Jesus (Matthew 4:10)

———ɷɷ———

O
ut in this desert place, a low, rumbling growl arises, waking Me from a fitful slumber against a bed of rocks. I get up with a start, thinking a wild animal has its sights set on Me. However, the further I move from the area of the noise, the louder it seems to grow. Finally, it occurs to Me: The sound is not coming from a mountain lion or jackal; rather, it is coming from My own stomach!

I have been out in the wilderness for the past forty days, and I am starving. My stomach feels as hollow as an empty spice jar. My mouth and throat feel like tanned leather from lack of water. I have had frequent headaches and dizzy spells for weeks on end. This deprivation has gotten to the point where I am not able to vomit or relieve Myself to alleviate these pangs, as there is nothing in My system to remove. It is by the grace of God, My Father, and the Holy Spirit, My Helper, that I am still alive.

It is good for Me to be out here, though. It has given Me a place and time to think and speak to God after My baptism and ordination. Since He first spoke to Me in the temple eighteen years ago, I have been anxiously waiting to receive His plans for My life. I lean against the trunk of a dying acacia tree to continue My thinking and praying.

During these forty days, My Father has revealed to Me some of what My last three years on this earth will entail. According to Him, I will perform many miracles and make many followers even more enemies. These enemies will eventually kill Me. My Father also says that My death has been part of His plan to redeem mankind from the very beginning.

When the forbidden fruit—the emblem of knowledge never meant for human beings—was taken, it introduced sin, pain, heartbreak, death, and other horrors associated with the separation from My Father. And Satan, oh that Satan, that cowardly snake, was behind all of it!

—◦◦◦—

Satan was not always a devil, an enemy of My Father. When he was first created, Satan, then called Lucifer, was one of My

21

Father's most beautiful angels. His surname, in fact, was Bright Morning Star.[12] Everywhere he went, Lucifer's luminous smile lit up the whole room and we—the rest of the angels and I— could not help but smile as well. He was also the strongest and most powerful angel, always ready and willing to do whatever was asked of him by My Father. One could not help but love Lucifer.

That is, until that fateful day when we heard him muttering to himself, "I will ascend to the heavens; I will raise my throne above the stars of God; I will sit enthroned on the mount of assembly, on the utmost heights. I will ascend above the tops of the clouds; I will make myself like the Most High."[13]

Somehow, Lucifer was able to convince one-third of the rest of the angels to join him in his plans to overthrow My Father. Of course, My Father, who knows all things, knew of this vile scheme even before they had come up with a plan of execution. After a terrific battle, Our archangel Michael, and all the rest of the angels who did not join Lucifer, conquered Lucifer and his angels and sent them spiraling down to the earth.[14] Oh, the

---

[12] See Isaiah 14:12

[13] See Isaiah 14:13b-14

[14] See Revelation 12:4, 7–9

22

screams! Oh, the swiftness of their falls! They were as bolts of lightning from heaven, heading straight for the Garden of Eden.

There, Lucifer, now Satan, disguised himself as an unassuming serpent, coiled around the tree of the knowledge of good and evil. Because My Father had thwarted his plan to become like Him, Satan decided to thwart My Father's creation of humankind by deceiving them into thinking *they* could become like Him.[15]

—◦◦◦—

Tears prick My eyes as I think about all the beauty, all the perfection, and all the closeness to My Father that humanity forfeited because of this serpent's lies. Knowing My thoughts, My Father comforts Me, saying, "I know, My Son. I know. This is the very reason I have sent You here. Your mission is to thwart Satan's power once and for all and win My creation back to Me. But I must warn You that it will cost You greatly. Yes, even Your very life. Only in sacrificing Your perfect, sinless life will You receive Your eternal glory and honor. Through You, humankind shall be saved."

"And what makes You so sure that Your grand plan will be successful, *o Great One?*"

---

[15] See Genesis 3:1–5

Suddenly, a new voice makes itself evident.

I turn towards the source of the voice, even as I know fully well whom the speaker is. Who I see is a tall, broad-shouldered figure dressed in a purple robe and fine linen with a golden sash. Around his neck is a golden chain that shimmers in the sunlight. His nails are like the claws of a lion, his teeth like the venomous fangs of a viper. Gleaming green, half-lidded eyes peer out through thick, flowing, dark hair. As he moves toward Me, he swings his hips and gives a bright, winning smile. Suddenly, he puffs out his brawny chest to let out an enormous yawn. As he yawns, I note the rich aromas of fine wine, fresh-baked bread, and date cakes on his breath. There is no mistake: I am in the presence of the great adversary, the old serpent, Satan himself.

"So, Jesus," Satan speaks again after he finishes yawning, his voice rich and deep like the purr of a young lion. "That was some big display down by the Jordan last month, wasn't it? The Big Man called You His 'beloved Son' whom He 'loves and is well pleased with.' Is that right?"

"What do you want, Satan?" I ask, though I am not interested in what Satan has to say.

Satan moves a bit closer to Me, in a slinking, fluid movement, until we are at eye-level. His eyes now have a softened expression, a perversion of kindness and concern, in them. "Are You *really* the Son of God?" he asks. "Would God really want His beloved Boy to go hungry and dehydrated? Any other man would have surely died by now. Tell You what ... "

Here, he stoops and picks up a stone. "If God really loves You and regards You as His Son, command this stone to become a loaf of bread to satisfy your hunger. Think of it: Warm, soft bread as if fresh out of the oven! It can all be Yours this very moment!"

He drops the stone into the palm of My hand and waits to see what I will do. Admittedly, the thought of food sounds wonderful right now and Satan's temptation is indeed quite strong. But then I hear the gentle voice of My Father saying, "No, My Son. You have nothing to prove to anyone here; not to Me, not to Satan, not to Yourself. You know that I love You. You know it in Your heart, yes, in Your very soul. Do not worry about when You will eat next. I have provided for You before and I will provide for You again."

Strengthened by My Father's words, I stand up to Satan and declare, "Satan, you are right that I am starving. But to listen to you and make food for Myself now would be to ignore My Father's words of love and instruction. My Father has spoken in

His word, 'Man shall not live by bread alone, but by every word that comes from the mouth of God.'"

Upon hearing this, Satan puts a hand to his mouth to stifle another yawn. "Ho-hum, the old 'Quote the Scripture' game," he rolls his eyes in disinterest as he finishes. "Well, two can play at this. Watch!"

Satan waves his hand in front of him with a mighty swish and we are both whisked away at such a dizzying speed that I see stars. As My vision clears, I see that we are no longer in the wilderness, but on the top of Solomon's temple, overlooking the streets of Jerusalem.

"If You really were the Son of God," Satan still tries to plant doubt inside My head, "He wouldn't set You up to die. Now, if You just jump from here, You won't have to. Didn't Your Father ever tell You in His word, 'He will command His angels charge over You. They will carry You up in their hands before You hit Your foot on a stone.' If You just do this one thing for Yourself, You can prove to all those people down there, once and for all, that You are the Christ and they would never dream of killing You."

Before I can even process a thought, I again here the voice of My Father warning Me, "No, My Son. This is not the way. You *need* to die. You *need* to shed Your precious, innocent blood to save humankind. That is the only way."

I counter Satan's attack with the words, "Satan, didn't My Father ever tell *you*, 'Do not put the Lord, your God, to the test'? You may be good at *quoting* scripture, but not *obeying* it."

In reply, Satan gives a smirk and, with a wave of his hand, we are on the precipice of a high mountain. Another wave, and all the kingdoms of the world are before Me. I see lavish tables laden with bread, roasted fish, lamb, fruit, and fine wine; halls filled with dancing, scantily-clad women; rooms loaded with gold, precious stones, and fine spices; vineyards overflowing with plump, juicy grapes.

As I am viewing all of this, Satan slithers up behind Me and, after another yawn, hisses in My ear, "So, are You *still* certain about Your dear Father's love and plan to save all humankind? Why, *I* could love You more than *He* ever could. I could give You everything You see here *and more!* All You must do is bow down and worship me right here and now!"

By now, I am fed up with Satan's lies. I am well-armed with the love I have for My Father and My knowledge of My Father's love for Me, as I stand My ground, look My tempter straight in the eye, and command, in a firm, mighty voice, "Get behind

Me, Satan! My Father says in His word, 'Worship the Lord your God and serve Him alone!' My Father loves Me and has the best plan for Me. You, on the other hand, can never love anyone! You cannot comprehend My Father's love! You shudder at His very name! And it is perfect love that will bring your doom! Depart from Me, you cursed one!"

Suddenly, Satan's eyes burn an angry blood red, and he gives a shrill, jackal-like shriek as the ground beneath his feet opens up to swallow him whole. The horrific stench of evil and burning sulfur fills My nostrils and makes My eyes and sinuses burn. An even more horrific heat knocks Me to My knees. However, I know that this punishment is not for Me, but for My tempter. The last thing I see and hear before finally fainting from intense hunger, thirst, and heat is Satan falling from the opening in the earth down to his everlasting fire, cursing My Father and Me all the way down.

———෴———

When I come to My senses, I see that I am in the middle of a lush oasis, with springs of fresh water and extravagant fruit trees. For one moment, I think I am home, in heaven, but then I see angels descending from the clouds and landing under the trees near Me. One of them fills a golden basin with the water gushing freely from one of the springs and places it in front of Me. Too weak to speak, I simply nod My thanks and plant My face into the basin, gulping deeply. After drinking My fill, I have the strength to dump the remaining water over My head to clean Myself.

A group of My heavenly servants lays out a sheet laden with bread and olive oil, lentil cakes, roasted fish, and fresh fruit plucked from the trees. They gesture for Me to come and eat. Before digging into this bountiful feast, I bow My head and pray the words of My ancestor David:

"You prepare a table before Me in the presence of My enemies. You anoint My head with oil; My cup overflows. Surely goodness and mercy shall follow Me all the days of My life, and I shall dwell in the house of the Lord forever."[16]

---

[16] Psalm 23:5–6

CHAPTER 4

"Do not be afraid; for as of today, I will make you a fisher of men."
—Jesus (Luke 5:10b)

———❧———

After about an hour or so of resting and eating, **My** Father puts His hand on My shoulder and whispers, "It's time to go now, My Son." Feeling better and stronger than ever, I leap to My feet and say, "All right, Father. I am ready."

As I descend the mountain overlooking the town of Galilee, a twinge of uneasiness touches Me. "Father?" I ask.

"Here I am, My Son," My Father answers.

"What do I say to the people down there? Will anyone listen to Me? Will anyone choose to follow Me?"

"Fear not, My Son. I will give You the right words to say. As for followers, there will be many who will not have the faith or the understanding to follow where You lead. However, I have selected twelve individuals to be Your main disciples. These men will follow You everywhere You go. They will worship and love You. They will uphold Your identity in Me. They will also doubt You and hurt You deeply. One of them will even lead You to Your death. But fear not: I will be with You and will watch over both You and them."

By now, I am entering the village of Galilee. The marketplace is buzzing with activity. *I wonder where the men that My Father has chosen for Me are. Will I find them in the marketplace?*

I hear My Father speak again, "Yes, My Son. You will surely find a great deal of disciples here. However, I suggest that You start Your search at the docks. There, You will find the first of Your disciples."

As I approach the docks, I notice the strong smell of fish—both fresh-caught and lying out in the sun to ferment. I continue My stroll until I come to one dock that does not smell as strongly as the others. There, against the posts of the dock, is slumped a very discouraged, sleep-deprived, young man with broad shoulders and thick, matted dark hair and a beard. His biceps are huge from many years hoisting full fishing nets.

"Excuse Me, My friend. Could you spare a ride upon the sea?" I inquire upon approaching this man.

The young man's half-lidded eyes open a bit wider with surprise and he stammers, "Er ... all right. I'll let my brother Andrew know that we are going. My name is Simon, by the way."

"Pleased to meet you, Simon. My name is Jesus. Jesus Bar-Joseph," I say with a smile.

"Hmm, Jesus ... The name means 'Salvation.' Ha! Salvation is just what this rundown, Roman-ruled city needs," Simon grumbles under his breath as he rises to get his brother.

—∞—

We have been on Simon and Andrew's boat for a little over an hour before I turn to the duo of brothers and suggest, "Why don't we push a little bit farther out?"

Andrew answers, "All right. For what?"

I grin knowingly as I say, "Well, what else? Let us see if we can catch some lunch!"

Andrew and Simon exchange embarrassed glances before bursting into barks of bitter, sardonic laughter. "Ha-ha! Jesus, don't You know anything about fish and their ways?" Simon snickers. "There aren't any fish about this time of the day! They're all asleep! And besides that, we have been out all night and haven't gotten a nibble! It is hopeless!"

Unfazed by Simon's ridicule, I plead with him, "Come on, Simon; try it once more? Something tells Me you will be surprised this time."

Attempting to desist his laughter, Simon smirks and says, "All right, if you insist." With that, the nets are cast.

Not ten seconds after the two brothers throw the nets into the sparkling waters, they lurch forward, struggling and grunting. It is My turn to laugh as the nets snap and twang and Simon and Andrew begin hoisting them up, their arms strained. The nets they pull up are swarming and gleaming with fish of all colors and sizes.

The duo joins Me in My laughter, only this time their laughter is that of joy and exhilaration. They cannot contain their excitement and disbelief that their nets, which had been once barren and dead, are now fertile and teeming with life.

After a few moments, Simon's laughter turns to gasps of panic; the nets are growing too full and are about to break. He and Andrew whistle and holler at a nearby fishing boat, where three men are drifting:

"James! John! Zebedee! Help us out here, will you?"

James and John, another set of brothers, motion to their father, Zebedee, and all three men gawk at our miraculous catch of fish. They continue to stare in awe until Simon gives another pleading call; then they start rowing closer towards our boat.

Simon and Andrew hoist up the nets and sling them over Zebedee's boat. Finally, we make the long haul back to shore.

———◦◦◦———

After we have tied up Simon's and Andrew's boat, I wander onto the beach to make a small fire. As I am roasting some of the fish to make lunch, I look up and see Simon sitting on a rock, looking just as glum as he had been when we first met this morning. My heart breaks for him. He was so happy and full of energy in the boat; I wonder what has got him down again.

"Simon?" I ask, walking over to where he is sitting. "Is something wrong?" I try to comfort him by placing My hand onto his broad shoulder, but he flinches and turns away as though I have burned him.

I move closer and look into his ruggedly handsome face. When I do, I see that he has tears in his eyes. In a voice thick with emotion and shame, Simon utters, "Leave me, Lord. Why trouble Yourself with a sinful man as I? Look at me: I am a disgrace, a pathetic failure!"

"Ah, Simon. Why do you say such things?" I take him and pull him to My chest. He does not resist this time. I stroke his hair as sobs wrack his body. After a while, I speak to him tenderly in a voice barely above a whisper, "Do not be afraid, Simon. For as of today, I will make you a fisher of men. You do not understand what this means now, but you will surely understand later."

———∽∽∽———

By the time I finish helping Simon through his bout of emotion, the fish I have been preparing is ready to eat. Andrew, James, and John come over to us, and together, we eat and get to know each other a bit more. I explain My mission, and after a while, I invite them to leave their livelihoods behind to follow Me. I do not have to ask twice; they agree with enthusiasm and great joy.

Later that evening, we stroll back out to the marketplace to find more of My disciples. I pass by the booth of a tax collector, but I have the sudden urge to go back.

"Yes, My Son, You are right. I have selected this despised and reviled tax collector to be Your disciple. His name is Levi. However, his name shall no longer be *Levi,* attached to the lusts and greed of this world, but *Matthew,* because he will be a gift and a blessing to both You and the rest of Your disciples," My Father speaks to Me, encouraging Me to invite him into My circle of followers.

"You there. Levi, is it?" I call out to him. The man cringes and crouches lower behind his booth in a vain attempt to hide. I smile with pity. The man must think I have stopped to curse at him.

"Ah, Levi. Do not be afraid. I have not come to yell or curse. I have come to offer My friendship to you and invite you to leave all this behind and follow Me."

Now Levi gives Me a look of both confusion and glad hopefulness. "Y-, You really mean it, Sir?" he asks, his voice trembling.

"Absolutely I do, My friend!" I exclaim with excitement.

"Yes, I-, I mean, of course! I'd love to!" Levi, now Matthew, sweeps all the shekels and mites he had been counting off his table and takes My hand. "Let's celebrate at my house tonight," Matthew says with a hearty laugh.

My four other disciples, Simon, Andrew, James, and John, smile in feigned politeness to Matthew's face, but once behind his back, their smiles turn to frowns of anger and incredulousness.

"Jesus," Simon hisses, "what are You thinking inviting that greedy, Roman-groveling slime-ball Levi? What will people think of You? What will they think of *us?*"

"Simon," I whisper gently yet firmly, looking Simon straight in the eye, "do not worry about what people will think. I am not worried. I have not come to invite the good, elite, perfect folk to follow Me. I have come to call the poor, the sinful, the downtrodden of society. You and your friends were but lowly fishermen this morning when I called you. Did you not say so yourself that you were a sinful man? I told you that I could still use you for My mission. Should I not extend the same grace and invitation to our friend *Matthew?*"

—⁓⁓—

Before heading to Matthew's house for supper, we continue our search in the marketplace for the rest of My disciples. There is Philip with his friend Nathanael. "Greetings, Nathanael! You faithful Israelite in whom there is no deceit," I call out as I take Nathanael's hand in My own.

"Lord, how do You know my name?" Nathanael asks.

"Because I saw you sitting under a fig tree yesterday. Philip was just about to come to you to tell you about Me."

Nathanael's face goes white, and he begins shaking violently. "Lord, you are the Son of God! You are the King of Israel!"

I chuckle and pat him on the back to calm him. "Why do you say that now? Just because I said that I saw you under the fig tree? Trust Me, Nathanael; you will see even greater signs and wonders than that! Why, you will even see heaven open and the angels of God ascending and descending on the Son of Man."

Nathanael stops shaking, but his eyes are still full of both fear and great excitement. "Like our father Jacob saw,"[17] he murmurs.

I look into his eyes and mimic an offended look. "And you asked if anything good could come from Nazareth."

Nathanael hangs his head in shame. "Forgive me, Lord. I spoke too soon."

I wink and clap him on the back. "All is forgiven, My friend! Come, join My circle!"

—◦◦◦—

Next, I call Thomas, Thaddeus, another man named James, and a zealot named Simon. I am up to eleven disciples now. Where could My twelfth be? Suddenly, a flash of red catches the corner of My eye, and a tall, thin young man with the smallest trace of a beard turns and approaches Me. As I look into his face, I notice a familiar pair of vivid green eyes amid wavy, shoulder-length black hair. *Where have I seen such eyes before?*

"Sir? Are You all right?"

The young man's concerned voice interrupts My musing. "Er, yes, My friend, I am fine. My name is Jesus Bar-Joseph. I am recruiting disciples, and I could use one more."

---

[17] See Genesis 28:10–19

The man comes closer and takes My hand. "It would be an honor, Sir!"

"Good! That makes twelve disciples all together! May I ask what your name is?"

"My name is Judas. Judas Iscariot," My newest disciple answers, then eagerly asks, "Is it true what they are saying about You? Are You really the One that we've been hoping and waiting for?"

I smile and say, "Well, follow Me and you shall see for yourself."

CHAPTER 5

"Your faith has healed you. Go in peace."
Jesus (Mark 5:34)

———※———

After lunch one day, Simon clears his throat and says, "Er, Jesus? Could I ask a favor of You?"

I answer, "Well, sure, Simon. What is it?"

"Well, you see, my mother-in-law is very ill with a raging fever. The doctors say that it isn't fatal, but my wife and I are still very worried."

"And you want Me to come over to her place and see if there is anything I can do for her? Do you really believe I can?"

At this, Simon gives a grin and says, "Well, I am not completely certain, but if You can help us catch a school of fish so large that it nearly breaks our nets without having any experience in fishing, there's no telling what else You can do."

I smile back at My first disciple as I take his hand. "All right, My friend. Lead Me to your house and to your mother-in-law. I will see what I can do."

———◈◈◈———

As I walk inside Simon's house, I note the quiet and stillness. The only sound I detect is the muffled sound of shallow breathing. I enter the room where the ailing woman is lying. She is ashen and pale, with flushed cheeks and disheveled hair that is sticking to her forehead, damp with sweat. Her lips are dry and chapped from panting. When her eyes fall on Me, she flushes deeper, half in surprise and half in embarrassment for allowing Me to see her in this state.

I am not embarrassed by her, however. I motion for her to lie back down. I smile down at her sympathetically, stoop down, and begin brushing her hair from her forehead. As I feel the heat radiating off her head, My heart sinks. Lifting My hand from her face, I pray deep inside My heart for My Father's help. Suddenly, I shiver as I feel My right hand grow rather cold, even in the warm sun streaking through the window. A thrill of hope surges through Me. *I wonder ...*

Hoping for the best, I lay the palm of My hand across the sick woman's forehead. "Mmm, feels good," she moans.

The words that come out of My mouth next are the rebuking words of "Fever, I command you to leave this woman alone, in the name of My Father in heaven!"

As soon as the final word leaves My lips, the woman gives a violent shiver. As her shivering subsides, the people in the room and Myself see the flush in her cheeks fade as the rest of her color returns. She gives a gasp of shock and excitement. "Oh my!" she utters as she motions Simon and his wife to her side. "My children, I think I am healed!" Turning to Me now, she goes silent for a moment. "Sir," she finally says, "it seems that You have healed me with Your touch and Your words."

"Woman," I say with a smile, "please, call Me Jesus."

She smiles back as she springs out of her bed. "Now that I am well, let's eat! You men make yourselves at home while I get you some wine."

I watch her skip out of the room, My heart pounding with joy inside My chest. I feel My Father smiling on Me and hear His voice saying to Me, "This is just the beginning, My Son."

"Lord, who sinned?" Simon asks, not even trying for discretion. "Who sinned, this man or his parents, that caused him to be born blind?"

I lower My eyes to stare lovingly into those of poor Bartimaeus. His eyes have been rolled back into his skull since birth, his face pale from avoiding the sun's rays. This young man has suffered all through his life. True, it is the result of

Satan's oppression, but Bartimaeus himself had done nothing to deserve this condition. How could he? He had not even been born yet. Therefore, I cannot help but feel stung by My best friend and disciple's remark.

In a stern voice, I mutter, "Listen, Simon. No one sinned. Not Bartimaeus; not his mother; not his father."

My tone softens as I speak as though addressing Bartimaeus as well as Simon. "This has simply happened so that God's glory and power may be displayed."

Turning directly to Bartimaeus himself, I take My hand and lift up his head so that his eyes meet Mine. "Bartimaeus," I whisper, as though about to reveal a great secret just for him.

"Mmm? What?" the blind young man mumbles, in a voice that conveys that he does not know what to expect to hear.

I grin from ear to ear as I continue to whisper, "Do you believe I can make you whole?"

Bartimaeus gives a deep, soft gasp, and now he is grinning with such intensity that even his eyes seem to light up. "Oh Lord, I believe! Yes, I believe!" he exclaims.

I laugh as I say, "All right, I will make you well. But I must warn you: it will take a little time."

"Oh Lord, I'd wait forever to be able to see!"

I utter another chuckle as I bend over, quickly work up a bit of saliva, and drool over a patch of dirt by My feet. When I feel the mud is moist enough, I knead and flatten it into a paste and smear it over Bartimaeus' eyes. "Now go wash off in the pool of Siloam and open your eyes."

Bartimaeus does as he is told and comes back to Me. "Well, what do you see?" I ask.

"Well, Lord," he answers, "I see people. But they look more like walking trees to me."

"Yes, I know. I told you before that it would take a little time. Do you still believe?"

"Oh most certainly I do, Lord!" the young man nods in enthusiasm.

I smile. "Good! Now close your eyes for a little while."

Bartimaeus closes his eyes as I press his eyelids with My thumbs and gently rub them in a circular motion. After about a half a minute, I remove My thumbs and command, "Now open them. What do you see?"

Bartimaeus' eyes slowly open, and he rapidly flutters them in pleasant surprise. He breaks into a smile and cries out in a combination of emotion and laughter, "Why, I see You! You and

Your disciples! You fellows don't look like trees at all. You look like … like … people!"

The man's now clear, seeing eyes well up with tears, and he covers his face with his hands. Emotion overtakes Me as well. Within a moment, we collapse into each other's arms, laughing and weeping with joy as My disciples look on in awe.

As I wander about the perimeters of the synagogue, My disciples come out to meet Me. Judas calls out, "Lord, have You heard? Bartimaeus has been expelled from the synagogue!"

My eyes widen. "Has he really? Why?"

"He was proclaiming to everyone about being able to see. When the Pharisees and teachers of the law heard about this and asked him how it happened, he told them that it was Your doing. Even his parents were brought in for interrogation."

Oh, how sad for Bartimaeus! I do hope this expulsion did not steal away the joy he had this morning. Did I do wrong in healing him at this time?

As I take the news in, I feel My Father's hand on My shoulder. "Fear not, My Son. This is not Your fault. I am well pleased with what You have done for Your friend Bartimaeus. Go, find him and reveal Your identity as the Son of Man[18] to him. He will believe in and worship You as such."

Just as I turn the corner, I nearly walk into Bartimaeus, who had been strolling about, enjoying the sun for the very first time in his life.

"Ah, Bartimaeus, I heard about what happened earlier. I am sorry."

"Ah no, don't be, Lord. I have a whole life of seeing ahead of me! That's all that matters," the man says cheerfully.

I smile at Bartimaeus' gladness as I look him in the eye and say, "Bartimaeus, do you believe in the Son of Man?"

Bartimaeus' eyes light up at My question. "You know the Son of Man! He has finally come? Where is He? Who is He? Tell me so that I may go and believe in Him!"

My smile broadens and I say plainly, "You are looking at Him. I am He!"

As evening approaches, we make our way back to Simon's house. After all the excitement of the day, I am tired and hungry. I look forward to the meal that Simon's mother-in-law has prepared for us. We sit down to eat, but no sooner has the food

---

[18] See Daniel 7:13–14; used here as a divine name for the Messiah

been passed around than we hear the sound of scraping mud above our heads. Soon, a cascade of dust and debris falls from the roof. We cautiously lift our eyes and, to our shock, there is a large, gaping hole in the roof and four men peering down through it. The men look frantic, but their expressions relax as their gazes fall upon Me. Using a rope, they lower a fifth man on a mat through the opening and down to the floor right beside the table where we are reclining.

I can see that this man suffers from paralysis: his limbs are limp as wet reeds from inactivity, his head is laid over his shoulder, his eyes clouded with hopelessness and pain. The familiar pang of anger and sorrow fills My soul. This is the result of sin and Satan's oppression upon humankind.

No more of this!

"Take comfort, My son," I whisper, looking tenderly into the young man's eyes. "Your sins are now forgiven."

No sooner has the final word left My lips than a fierce, ominous murmuring arises. It starts out soft, like the wings of a locust, then grows louder, into a grumbling rumble so loud it makes My ears ache. As it starts to desist, I am better able to make out words:

"Sins? Forgiven?"

"Blasphemer!"

"Only God has the authority to forgive sins."

Now I know the source of all this commotion. It is coming from the minds and hearts of the religious leaders, the Pharisees. I face towards them, My face stony and determined.

"What is all this grumbling?" I ask. The Pharisees look at one another in confusion, as they have not even opened their mouths.

"Which is easier to say?" I continue. 'Your sins are now forgiven' or to say, 'Get up and walk'?"

The expression doesn't leave the Pharisees' faces as they focus their eyes off of each other and back onto Me, eyebrows raised in incredulousness.

"But to prove to you that the Son of Man has the authority on earth to forgive sins ..." I break into a smile, turn on My heels, and direct My attention back to the man lying on the mat. He smiles back at Me a bit nervously, but there is now a glimmer of hope in his eyes.

"I command you: Pick up your mat and go home. Your faith has made you well. Your faith and the faith of your four friends."

At first, the man just looks around the room, an unsure expression on his face. *What if it didn't work? What if he falls, in front of all these people?*

Enough what ifs! I take him by both hands and slowly raise him up. The young man is so surprised, he nearly stumbles to his knees. But then, he gives a gasp of shock as the muscles in his feet and legs feel strength and health rush through them. He gives a small, experimental hop just to be sure. Then a bigger jump. Then a wide leap with great gusto.

"Oh, my friends," he cries, lifting his head towards the hole in the roof. "You were right! This Man can heal anyone! And He did! Watch!"

He begins to skip and run in place now. On the roof, his friends give a loud cheer and slap their hands against each other's. Soon, the whole room is filled with joy, and everyone cries out in ecstasy. Everyone, that is, except the Pharisees.

Some time later, it is My turn to lead the teaching in the synagogue. I open the scroll and begin reading from it:

"But those who wait upon the Lord shall renew their strength. They shall mount up with wings like eagles. They shall walk and not grow weary; they shall run and not faint."[19]

Suddenly, a woman in the crowd catches My attention. This is a woman who has been crippled and hunched over for eighteen years now. My heart fills with compassion for her. I know that is the Sabbath and that I should not do what I am about to. Nevertheless, I motion for her to come forward. Puzzled, she looks around to see if I had addressed someone else. Seeing no one respond to My call, she abashedly makes her slow, feeble way to the front of the congregation.

When the woman becomes too weak to take another step, I come meet her the rest of the way. My hand cups her gently on the back as I say, "Woman, you are set free from your infirmity." I then put My other hand on her shoulder and slowly press up so that her shoulders and back are perfectly aligned.

The woman's eyes widen with joy as she stands straight and tall and raises her hands in front of the crowd to show them what has just occurred. "I am cured! Praise God! Hallelujah," she declares. Her praises echo off the walls of the synagogue as the

---

[19] Isaiah 40:31

people stare in silent wonder. The religious leaders, however, are not pleased.

Breaking the glorious silence, the synagogue leader's indignant voice thunders, "Six! Six days to get work done in a week! If one wishes to heal or to be healed, they ought to come on those six days! Why do you allow this Fellow to corrupt the peace and rest by healing this woman on the Sabbath?" Behind him, the Pharisees and the teachers of the law sneer and nod their heads in agreement.

A feeling of guilt weighs on Me as I hang My head and pray, "Forgive Me, Father. I have sinned."

"No, My Son. You have not," I hear My Father speak tenderly to Me. "It is this corrupt generation of teachers and Pharisees who have taken My perfect laws and used them to oppress the very people the rules were made to help. You have not sinned; You could never sin. I would not have sent You here if I knew that You would."

Encouraged by My Father's words, I stand up to the leader and his team and shout, "Hypocrites! Doesn't each of you on the Sabbath untie your ox or donkey from the stall and lead it out to give it water? Then should not this woman, a daughter of

Abraham, whom Satan has kept bound for eighteen long years, be set free on the Sabbath day from what bound *her?"*

As the echoes of My last words die down, the crowd erupts with applause and cries of acclamation and praise. But the religious leaders go silent, seething with rage and humiliation. I have a feeling that this is not the last time our ways will clash.

———∕∕∕———

I take My disciples and we head back to Simon's house. Though it is only midday, I find Myself feeling weary and discouraged at heart. All this time, I have been healing and showing God's love to those around Me, yet somehow, I manage to rouse the anger of the Pharisees. I am beginning to have My doubts; am I going about this the wrong way?

Suddenly, a man bursts through the door of his house in a frenzy and starts to approach us. I recognize him as Jairus, another leader of the synagogue.[20] It seems as though he has been watching from the window for Me for a while now. A slight feeling of apprehension touches Me. I wonder what the nature of this encounter will be. Has he come to rebuke or ridicule Me for My recent actions?

---

[20] Not to be confused with the synagogue leader who rebuked Jesus for healing on the Sabbath

However, there is no fury or glare in this man's eyes—only tears of sorrow and intense fear. When he finally reaches us, he falls on his knees in reverence and petition before Me.

"Rabbi![21] Rabbi Jesus!" Jairus begins, panting from exertion. "Please come to my house! It is my darling little girl! She is very ill! She's been ill for weeks, and she is only twelve years old. She should not be suffering through this. But I believe You can make her well again."

Now, My own eyes fill with tears of love and compassion for this father who truly loves and values his daughter. "Oh Jairus, of course I will come. Take Me to your little girl."

Jairus gives a small smile of hope and gratitude as he takes My hand and starts to lead Me to his home where the child is lying. By now, however, a large crowd has gathered from all sides of My disciples and Me. People have heard of what I have been doing lately and wish to catch a glimpse of Me. Unfortunately, this crowd makes it hard for Me to move very quickly.

To make matters worse, a sensation of exhaustion suddenly overtakes Me. I feel as though I have been jogging for

---

[21] Jesus was actually a carpenter by trade. Because He often taught in the Temple and synagogues, He was referred to as "Rabbi," but He was never officially ordained as one.

a whole hour. My shoulders heave as I double over, panting and sweating.

Jairus stops and asks, "Rabbi, what happened?" Through gritted teeth, I groan, "Wh-, who touched Me?"

Simon gives a guffaw and says, "Lord, just look at the crowd! I would say that the whole village is touching and pressing upon You!"

I shake My head. "No, Simon. This touch was different. I felt power flow out from Me. This means that someone in the crowd has been made whole by touching Me. Who was it?"

Through the crowd, a woman peeks her head out. Barely making eye contact, she speaks in a whimper that conveys great fear but also great joy:

"Forgive me, Lord. It was I who touched You. I have been bleeding for twelve long years.[22] The healers' treatments have only made it worse. I heard about You giving sight to blind Bartimaeus and restoring the back of the woman in the synagogue. But, by the time I arrived to find You, this crowd had grown too large. It took the last bit of strength I could muster

---

[22] Most biblical scholars interpret this bleeding to be menstrual bleeding. The people would have understood this affliction to be very detrimental to a woman's social and religious life, as it rendered her ritually unclean.

to reach out and touch the end of Your robe. I knew in my heart that just the touch of You would make me whole, and it did!"

My heart softens as I lift up her head and peer into her eyes. "Oh, My daughter, your faith has made you well! Go in peace!"

I kiss her lightly on the hand and watch her eyes fill with tears of joy as she smiles and scurries off to tell her friends and family.

By now, Jairus is antsier than before. He tugs at My sleeve and urges, "Er, Lord, this is all very good, but we really must hurry if my little girl is going to survive."

My strength has been replenished, so I nod and continue wading through the crowd to Jairus' house. As we are walking, I hear, unheard by Jairus, a deep, ghastly exhalation, silence, and finally weeping and frantic voices. *Oh no, I'm too late! The girl is dead.*

I am about to weep when I feel My Father's hand on My shoulder and hear His voice speaking, "No, My Son. You are not too late. Remember that I have placed all authority of life and death into Your hands. Now is the time to use it!"

Not long after My Father has finished speaking, a flute dirge sounds, and two men bearing grave countenances step out the door and approach us. "No use bothering the Rabbi now, Master. Your daughter has already passed."

Upon hearing this news, Jairus hangs and shakes his head. He then looks Me hard in the face as if to say, "*How could You? How could You stop to help a shameful, common woman when You were supposed to help me? Me, a holy man! A leader of the synagogue! I trusted You, and You let my little girl die! How could You?*"

I stare back into his face and softly say, "Do not be afraid, Jairus. Just keep on believing. Your daughter will be made well; I promise you."

Jairus sighs and nods his head slowly. He takes My hand and leads Me into his house. Inside is a bustle of noise: The girl's mother is weeping while packing up her daughter's belongings in preparation for burial. The funeral players are carrying on with their feigned grief and mourning.

"All right, that is enough!" I declare loudly enough to be heard by the whole room. "Why all this ruckus? This child is not dead; she is only sleeping."

I, of course, know that the little girl is dead. I merely meant that she wouldn't be dead for much longer. The mother ceases her packing and weeping and turns to Me, her red-rimmed eyes wide with surprise and confusion at My words. The players also gawk at Me for a moment before exploding into teasing laughter.

"Now, get out!" I yell at the mockers. Shoving them out the door, I beckon Simon, James, and John inside in their place.

Sure enough, there, lying in the bed, is the pale, limp body of the twelve-year-old child. I march up to the bed, run My fingers through her lank, dark hair, unkempt from many weeks in bed, and whisper, "It is time to wake up, little girl."

I motion Jairus and his wife over to the bed. They approach their daughter's bedside, shaking and hardly daring to believe what is occurring before their eyes. The once-dead girl's shoulders begin wriggling as she yawns and stretches, the color returning to her face. She rubs her eyes and sits up. Adjusting her eyes to her surroundings, her gaze falls upon Me.

"Sir," she murmurs groggily as if woken up from a nap. "Are You the Rabbi everyone's been talking about?"

I smile warmly at her as I answer, "Why yes, My dear child. I am."

The girl looks around a bit more and notices her belongings scattered on her bed and piled up near the door. "What are my things doing sitting out?" she demands, still seeming half asleep.

At their daughter's question, her father Jairus and her mother break down in a mixture of tears and laughter. "Mama, Papa, why are you crying? What's happened?" By now, the girl is wide awake, and she leaps out of bed to comfort her parents.

"Your parents will explain everything later, child," I say.

As the girl puts her arms around her parents and kisses them, I hear her stomach give a growl. "Jairus, I believe your daughter is hungry. You should get her something to eat." Jairus, giddy with shock and great joy, nods and turns to the kitchen for a loaf of bread.

I feel the hollowness of My own stomach and motion to Simon, James, and John that it is time to go. Before we head out the door, however, I call behind Me, "Oh, one more thing, Jairus: Please do not mention this to anyone."

CHAPTER 6

"For God so loved the world that He gave His one and only Son,
that whosoever believes in Him shall not perish but have eternal life."
—Jesus (John 3:16)

———❧———

T he breeze is blowing lightly across the banks of the
Jordan, making the grass and reeds dance and sway as
if in a little rendezvous. I sit alone with My thoughts and My
Father, the sky above Us fading to deep bluish-purple along
the horizon.

"You have done well, My Son," My Father begins.

"Thank You, Father," I answer, "for helping Me accomplish
all those miracles."

"Oh My Son, this is just the beginning," He continues.
"Through You, many more will be set free from the bondage
of Satan's tyranny. I have searched Your heart and know Your
love and compassion for humankind. I also know of Your dis-
couragement and weariness brought on by the opposition of
the religious leaders. And yes, Your perception is correct: these

leaders will continue to revile You and reject Your love. Many of them will even be involved in Your death. However, I have planted seeds of openness to understand inside the hearts of a few. One of them is on his way to speak with You this very moment. His name is Nicodemus."

—⟶⟶⟶—

Nicodemus. I remember him. He was with the other Pharisees and teachers of the law the day they brought Me a woman that they claimed to have caught in the act of adultery. But wait: Where is the man[23] who was also with her? Something doesn't seem right here. Could they perhaps be trying to trick Me?

Looking down, I see the woman struggling against the religious leaders' grasps and crying out in fear. Her head is bowed low so as to not make eye contact with Me, thinking she will only see anger and disapproval on My countenance. But she is wrong. Rather than anger and disapproval, I have nothing but pity and love and pardon for her. No, My anger is directed at the religious leaders and their self-righteousness.

---

[23] In Levite law, both the woman and the man who were caught in an adulterous act needed to be brought out and stoned, not just the woman (see Deuteronomy 22:22).

"Teacher!" one of the Pharisees barks. "This woman was caught in the act of adultery. In the Law, Moses commanded us to stone such women. Now, what do You say?"

Aha ... the Pharisees are trying to trick Me! Two can play at this. I grin, stoop down, and begin writing in the sand in front of the woman's face. When the woman sees what I am writing, she looks into My face, sees My confident yet gentle grin, and slowly gives a small, hopeful smile.

"Teacher!" another Pharisee snaps. "Quit fooling around and tell us what to do!"

I stand up straight and say coolly, "Listen, I will allow the man among you who is without sin to throw the first stone at her."

The Pharisees' faces drop when they hear My words, and they begin looking around to see if one of them would pick up that first stone. Upon seeing this, I chuckle quietly and begin writing again in the sand. Finally, the Pharisees shake their heads and begin walking away, beginning with the oldest among them, the stones falling from their hands like unripe figs from a tree.

I lightly touch the shoulder of the woman, who is still watching Me write. When she looks up, to her surprise, she sees that there is no one else around except for Me.

"Woman, where did they all go? Is no one condemning you now?"

"No one, Sir," the woman says with a relieved smile.

"Nor do I condemn you," I say, pulling her closer to Myself and kissing her tenderly on the forehead before sending her off with the warning, "Go now, and sin no more."

Nicodemus was that Pharisee who had left the circle first.

———∽∽∽———

"Rabbi? Rabbi Jesus? Is that You?" Here he comes, the white on his tassels flapping in the wind, glowing under the light of the moon. He seems excited to find Me. I wonder what he desires to speak with Me about.

I rise and go to meet him, smiling politely. "Ah, you must be Nicodemus."

"Er, yes. I am Nicodemus," the older man replies, a bit surprised that I already know his name.

"Tell Me, what brings you out here this late at night?"

"Well ... er ..." Nicodemus rocks back and forth on his heels anxiously. "I just wanted to talk with You in private for a while. First of all, I would like to extend an apology for my comrades' hostility lately. I want You to know that while there are many of us who have our doubts about You, there are also some of us who truly believe that You are a prophet sent by God. Healing crippled women? Raising children from the dead? No ordinary man could do the things that You have done."

I smile again, uplifted by the Pharisee's words. "Yes, you are correct about that, Nicodemus. Come, sit with Me awhile." Nicodemus approaches closer to where I have been seated, and sits cross-legged next to Me.

"Nicodemus, I can see that you truly want to see the coming of the Kingdom of God." Nicodemus' eyes light up as he nods. "Well," I say somberly, "Unless one is born again, he cannot see it."

At these words, Nicodemus' face falls and takes on an expression of disappointment and perplexity. "Ah, Rabbi," he bemoans, "How can a man be born again, much less an old man like myself? I cannot just crawl back inside my mother's womb. That is impossible!"

I laugh heartily at the mental picture as I put My hand on Nicodemus' shoulder in a calming manner. "No, no, My friend. You misunderstand My point. What I meant was that one cannot fully experience the kingdom of God unless they are born of both water and spirit: Both a physical birth and a spiritual birth. Baptism." Here, I wave My hand in front of Nicodemus' face, motioning towards the river.

I continue: "It is much the same as when one sees the grass sway in the wind. One cannot see the wind itself, but he or she knows it is there by the way it feels and the way it whispers and howls through the trees. In this way, it proves its presence and its power."

Nicodemus shakes his head at My words in awe and wonder. "How does the wind do all that?" he murmurs.

I turn and raise My eyebrow at him in incredulousness. "You are a teacher of the law. People look up to you because of your wisdom, yet you do not even understand the basic elements? I am talking to you about the simplest of subjects, and still you have no perception. How are you going to understand if I talk with you about the deep mysteries of God?"

Taken aback by My rebuke, Nicodemus hangs his head and says thickly, "Forgive me, Rabbi. I will pay attention. I truly do want to understand. Please continue."

I sigh greatly and nod. This man, blind as he is, is earnest about trying to understand the words I speak. My eyes soften as I say, "Very well, I shall go on. You remember the story of Moses' salvation of the Israelites in the desert? How God sent those venomous snakes to bite and punish them? Moses made the bronze snake and lifted it up, so that everyone who looked upon it would be saved from the poisonous bites."

Nicodemus nods. "Oh yes, I remember the story quite well."

I smile and continue, "Well, I *am* that snake! When the time comes, I too shall be lifted up, so that anyone who comes and looks upon Me shall be saved. You see, God loves this world. He has loved it from the very beginning. This love is so great that He has sent His one and only Son, Me, to make a way for anyone who believes in Me to live forever with Us and never die.

You Pharisees teach more about God's wrath and punishment. The truth is, God is not entirely the way you portray Him. He has not sent Me into this world to punish it, but to save it. Those who believe in Me need not fear condemnation, but those who do not believe are already condemned. Is this making any sense to you?"

Nicodemus furrows his eyebrows and remains silent for a few moments. Finally, he gives a sad, tired smile and shakes his head. "Rabbi, please don't be angry with me. I am trying so hard. You must know that I want, more than anything, to understand these beautiful, wonderful mysteries of Yours. But alas, I cannot!"

My heart softens for My friend as I drape My arm around his shoulder. "Do not be afraid, Nicodemus. I do not blame you for not understanding. Just remember that God loves you. He loves you so very much. Keep your heart and mind open to receive what He wants to reveal to you. If you do, one day, you will understand."

Nicodemus smiles and drapes his arm around Me in return. "Thank You, Rabbi, for Your kind words of wisdom."

He yawns now and looks out towards the horizon. The sky is utterly black now, except for the moon and a few stars. "Well, I don't wish to be the one to end our time together, but it is late."

I nod in affirmation. "So it is. It must be about ten o'clock by now."

"Yes," the older man continues. "And I have an early morning in the synagogue tomorrow. I must be heading off to bed."

"Of course, My good man," I say as I gently clasp Nicodemus' hand with My own. "I bid you goodnight."

"You as well, Rabbi," Nicodemus answers as he rises to go on his way.

As I watch him go, I pray, "Father, is there hope of understanding for this man?"

My Father frowns and furrows His eyebrows as if deep in thought. Finally, He breaks into a smile and answers, "Well, My Son, I will share with You two secrets about Our friend Nicodemus. Firstly, when the other Pharisees and teachers of the law speak ill of You to one another, Nicodemus will be Your greatest advocate.[24] And secondly, when You are finally at rest, Your ultimate work completed, Nicodemus will be the one to carry You to Your grave, burying You with seventy-five pounds of myrrh.[25] Do You know what great amount that is, My Son? That is the same amount that a *king* would be buried with! So, what do You think? *Is* there hope for Nicodemus? For ordinary men, his situation would seem impossible. But with Me, nothing is impossible."[26]

---

[24] See John 7:50

[25] See John 19:39

[26] See Matthew 19:26

CHAPTER 7

"Consider the ravens: They do not sow or reap,
they have no storeroom or barn; yet God feeds them.
And how much more valuable you are than birds!"
—Jesus (Luke 12:24)

"What kind of Man is this? Even the winds and the waves obey Him!"
—The disciples (Matthew 8:27)

———※———

T he days grow into weeks, which in turn bloom into several months, as the love and friendship between us deepens. I continue to teach My disciples about the ways of My Father's kingdom and My mission on earth. Sometimes they seem to understand, but not always.

Some of the people I have healed have taken to following after Me. One of them is named Mary of Magdalene. I cast seven demons out of her and have been teaching her to love and cherish herself the way I do. She has loved and followed Me since the day we first met. Of course, My mother sometimes joins Me on My travels, as well as her friends Johanna, Suzanne, and Salome, the wife of Zebedee.

Lately, My mind has been wandering back to My beloved cousin and baptist, John. He has been put into prison by King Herod for condemning Herod's marriage to his[27] brother's widow. The last I heard from My cousin was that he was beginning to have second thoughts about Me. He sent his disciples to Me asking if I really was the true Messiah, or if he should wait for someone else.

My heart aches over the fact that My cousin could be so on fire for Me one day and doubting Me the next. At the same time, I feel a thrill of excitement as I think back through all the miracles I have performed since we last saw each other. I tell John's disciples everything and have them deliver the message to John.

Today, I am awaiting John's reply. What could be racing through his head right now as he ponders My news?

Suddenly, My mother, her friends, and Mary Magdalene come running up the road towards Me, sobbing immensely while My main twelve follow alongside them, bearing somber, bereft expressions. My eyes widen as I try to deny the worst, and I dash over to meet them, crying, "No! No! Don't tell Me—"

Upon reaching Me, Mother takes Me into her arms as if I were a little child again and continues to cry into My chest.

---

[27] Herod's

As her crying dies down, she is able to articulate the words. "My Son, we've just gotten news from Jerusalem. Your beloved cousin, John the Baptist, has been beheaded by Herod."

Johanna explains to Me about the king's birthday feast and how his step-daughter danced in a way that so pleased him that he promised her anything she wanted. When she went to her mother, asking what to request, her mother told her to ask for John's head on a silver platter. Herod was very upset about this; he was angry with John, but did not want to harm him, as so many considered him a prophet. At the same time, he could not break his promise in front of his guests. It was with a heavy heart that Herod ordered that My cousin be beheaded and his head given to his step-daughter. In turn, she gave it to her mother.

Again, like a little child, I begin to cry now, as the truth of the matter sinks in. Mother continues to hold Me and stroke My hair as I do so. Finally, after a couple minutes, I manage to choke out, "Where is My cousin laid to rest?"

The twelve take Me to a plot of land where John is buried.

"Please, My friends, leave Me alone with him a while."

"Sure, take all the time You need," murmurs Andrew.

The men leave, and I am alone with the mound in the earth[28] that was once My cousin. The babe who leapt for Me before he was even born; the man whose mighty voice could drown out all the shofars in the temple; the prisoner who struggled with his doubts up to his death; now forever still, silent, and at peace.

Overcome with these memories and My grief, I feel My knees fall onto the dirt near the mound as I plead aloud, "Oh, Father, can't You ... Can't *I*—"

Before I even finish My thought, I already know what My Father's answer is going to be. I see Him sadly shake His head and drape His mighty arm around Me.

"No, I am sorry, My Son. I grieve for You that Your cousin is dead, but it was My timing. I gave him a special purpose in life, and he has fulfilled it. That purpose was to prepare You and prepare the way for You and to proclaim Your arrival to everyone who would listen. Now You are prepared and You have Yourself a great band of followers. What more could John ask?"

I heave a deep, shuddering sigh before answering, "Yes, Father, I know. But I miss John, Father. I miss him so much."

My Father says nothing, but holds Me tighter and gently rubs My back as My words trail off and give way to great sobs,

---

[28] The exact fashion in which John the Baptist was buried is unclear. See Matthew 14:12

wracking My frame. Finally, as My sobbing subsides, My disciples come to find Me.

"Jesus," Simon says, putting his own burly arm around Me, "we are deeply sorry about John. We know how important he was to You."

I nod silently. Suddenly, a thought comes to My mind. "Do you suppose John ever found out about what I have been doing lately?"

"Oh, I wouldn't doubt that," Thomas says with a hopeful smile. "News of You and Your miracles has been traveling throughout all of Israel. I bet even King Herod himself has heard. Perhaps John overheard when Chuza, Johanna's husband and Herod's chief official, reported to him."

"Yes, perhaps," I answer, still melancholy but comforted by My disciple's words. I rise and say, "Come. Let us go somewhere we can be alone together a while."

———⟡———

We settle into Simon and Andrew's boat and row out. After a couple of hours, we dock and begin to hike up a small hill. Just as we are almost to the top, our jaws nearly drop to the ground. There, in front of our eyes, is a great multitude of people! There must be about five thousand men, not even including the women and children.

"Er, Lord," Judas whispers to Me, fidgeting uncomfortably. "Didn't You say You wanted us to go off *alone?* What are we to do about this crowd?"

"Yes, My friend. I know what I said. Please give Me a moment to think this over," I answer gently to My restless disciple.

"Forgive Me, Father," I pray. "But I am at a moment of weakness. I just don't think I can do this right now."

My Father looks Me in the eye and gently yet firmly answers, "My Son, do not worry about Your weakened strength. This is what I want You to do. I want You to go to these people and minister to their needs. Then, when it is time, I will make a way for all to eat and be satisfied. If I ask You to do something, You must trust that I will give You the strength to obey. Now take Your disciples and go minister to My people."

I nod wearily. "Yes Father, I will obey."

Then, turning to My disciples, I state, "My friends, these people need Me now. Look at them; they are lost and lonely, like sheep without a shepherd. I must care for them. Many hearts will be restored through Me today. Just the thought lifts My own spirits a bit."

———ℰℰℰ———

And so it is. The whole day, I heal many people of their blindness, their lameness, even their demon possession. The demons come out, screaming at Me, "You are the Holy One of God!"

I tell them to be quiet, as My time has not yet come.

In between healings, I give the people words of wisdom and encouragement. "Do not worry, My friends, about what you will eat or drink or wear. Consider the ravens. Can they stroll out to the marketplace and buy themselves a bushel of grain? No, they cannot. They have no need; God provides them with what they need to live on each day. What about the lilies? Do you see them pulling out looms and thread and begin weaving? Certainly not. But then, how is it that they are clothed so richly that King Solomon would blush when beholding them? Why, God clothes them, of course! Is your life not dearer to God's heart than a whole flock of ravens or a whole field of lilies? So do not worry, My little flock; God will provide you with what you need each day."

———ℰℰℰ———

Before I know it, Simon taps My shoulder, saying, "Master, it is growing late, and the people must be starving. Let's send them home so they can eat their supper."

Those nearby who have overheard Simon's words nod and clutch their stomachs in agreement. However, I do not wish to send them away quite yet. My Father has promised to feed them through Me.

I answer, "Why must they go away? Surely we can find something for them to eat ourselves. Let us go among the crowd and see what we can find."

"But Lord," Philip cries in protest, "How are we ever going to find enough for everyone? Not even a year's wages would be enough to pay for this much food!"

"Er, Rabbi Jesus," a small voice pipes up behind Philip. There stands a young boy with a basket. "I'd like to share what I have. It's not much, though." He opens his basket. Inside, we see five round barley loaves and two smelt fish.

Upon eying this measly meal, Philip tries to hold back a laugh. "W-well, thank you, boy, very much for trying to help, but—"

"We will take it," I cut in with a grateful smile. "Let Me see what I can do."

The boy eagerly hands Me his basket, and I lift it up in My hand.

"Blessed are You, O Lord our God, who brings forth bread from the earth,"[29] I pray. Next, I have the people sit in groups of ten. Finally, I call the disciples forward to retrieve the food from Me to give to the people. As they do, I take the bread and break off as many pieces as I feel will suffice for each group. No matter how much I break off, I always have a full loaf of bread in My hand. The same thing happens with the fish. I fill the people's baskets with the food and send the disciples out among the groups to serve it to them. Soon, everyone is eating and being satisfied.

———

Even after everyone has eaten their fill, the bread and fish still haven't run out. Therefore, I take My disciples' empty food baskets and fill them up as well. The food doesn't start to run out until the last disciple's basket is full.

As My disciples rise to head back to the boat, I call after them, "You men go ahead. I have had a long and hard day, and I would like to spend some time in prayer. I will meet up with

---

[29] Traditional Jewish prayer and blessing

you later tonight." My disciples nod empathetically as they start to descend the hill.

As I bid farewell to the remainder of the crowd and send them home, I feel My spirit grow lighter than it has been all day. I sit down on the green grass and pray to My Father, "Oh Father, thank You for Your power in providing those people, Your flock, to satisfaction."

My Father smiles, places His hand onto My head, and answers, "My Son, it was You and Your willingness to obey, despite Your weakened spirit, that truly caused the miracle. This obedience and faithfulness to My will shall, one day soon, bring about the salvation of humankind."

At My Father's words, I go silent and somber for a few moments. It has been a while since I last truly thought about My ultimate purpose for being here. *Am I really ready to die?*

Reading My thoughts, My Father whispers tenderly, "Don't worry, My Son. I will tell You when the time comes. For now, I want You to continue doing what You have been doing: healing the sick, teaching Your disciples, and sharing My love with those around You. I will be sure that everything is ready for Your sacrifice. I love You, My Son."

"And I love *You*, My Father."

For a while, We sit, overlooking the lake, enjoying the coolness of the evening and the sunset. Soon, however, the once orange and pink skies grow unusually dark in a short period of time, and a cold, rapid wind starts blowing and howling through the trees. Eventually, the once smooth waters become white-capped waves. To make matters worse, I see My disciples right in the middle of the lake, with no shore nearby to swim to in the case of a shipwreck.

"Oh Father, My disciples! I must go help them!"

I have not considered how I can meet up with them, but now an idea forms in My head.

"Do You suppose I could ... ?" I ask with a grin, motioning to the lake.

My Father, upon eyeing the lake, gives a great, booming belly laugh and answers, "Now You've got it, My Son! Go now and comfort Your disciples!"

———❧———

Nodding, I sprint down the hill and approach the lake. I stick one foot in the water and, to My surprise, it does not sink through, but is supported by the water. Growing bolder, I stick My other foot into the lake. Now I am standing straight upon the water. The water is still wet and cold, of course, but somehow, it also feels solid.

This newfound power excites Me, but I know that this is no time to play around. I raise My eyes out in front of Me and see My disciples struggling and dumping water out of the boat so that it will not sink. Quickly, I make My way across to them. It is even easier to make good time because the waves carry Me along.

Upon setting eyes on Me, My disciples stare for a moment. Finally, Thomas lets out a scream and cries, "A ghost, men! A ghost!" Now all of My disciples are in a frenzy, panicking.

I chuckle a little, then call out, "Take courage, My friends! It is I, your Lord Jesus! Do not be afraid!"

I watch My disciples relax a bit, but their eyes are still filled with surprise at My ability to walk on water.

"Lord!" Simon calls out with enthusiasm and bravado. "Is that really You? If it is, tell me to come over to You on the water!"

"All right, Simon! Come on!"

Simon's eyes widen and he gives a gasp. Without waiting another second, he jumps feet-first out of the boat. As his feet hit the water, he gives a shout of shock and amazement and turns to face the other eleven still in the boat. They are staring in wonder at Simon, with a hint of jealousy.

Simon turns back to Me. With determination and faith, he comes sprinting towards My open hand. Sadly, as he is about to reach out to take My hand, a bolt of lightning flashes onto My face, and a thunderclap sounds. My heart nearly breaks in two as Simon's face falls and goes white. As if in slow motion, he takes his eyes off of Me and onto the rising waves. The moment he does, he sinks right through the raging, wild waters like a millstone.

Before his head goes under, he yelps, "Lord! Save me!"

I hurry to his aid, grab his hand, and help him to his feet. He comes up, shivering, sputtering, and clutching My robes.

"Ah, Simon. What little faith you have. Why have you doubted Me?" I rebuke gently and with great compassion. I hold him close now as his eyes well with tears; he begins to weep.

"Come, let us get you back into the boat and dried off."

I take his hand and lead him back to the others. As we climb back into the boat, I turn and whisper to the wind and waves, "Peace, be still."

In a heartbeat, the elements obey and desist. All is still. I turn to My other eleven disciples and ask sternly, "As for the rest of you, where is *your* faith? After everything you have seen today and all of the other miracles you have seen Me perform, do you still not trust Me?"

Upon hearing this, My disciples shrink back in shame and awe for a moment and then turn to each other, asking, "What kind of Man is He that we are following? Even the wind and the waves answer to Him!"[30]

---

[30] Literary license: These are actually two different stories. Simon's story is recorded in Matthew 14 and Jesus' story of calming the storm is found earlier on in Matthew 8. Here, the stories are combined for clarity.

CHAPTER 8

"Let the little children come to Me, and do not hinder them, for the Kingdom of God belongs to such as these. Truly I tell you, anyone who will not receive the Kingdom of God like a little child will never enter it."
—Jesus (Luke 18:15–17)

———❦❦❦———

H ow quickly time seems to go by lately. It must be almost three years since the beginning of My ministry. We are all the best of friends now. The disciples seem so happy and content following and learning from Me. A part of Me wonders how I am going to break the news about My departure from them.

I am relaxing near a sycamore tree, enjoying the warmth of the sun and watching the children laugh and play and roll about in the lush green grass. My mind wanders back to the days of laughing and playing in this very meadow with My cousin John. I feel a pang of sorrow and grief as I recall what became of him, and My eyes grow moist.

Suddenly, I hear crying, but it is not My own. It sounds higher-pitched and more child-like. I look behind the tree and see a little boy, his hands covering his face. My heart melts for the crying child, and I approach him.

"My dear boy, what has gotten you down today?" I ask him, tears of compassion in My eyes.

The boy stops his crying and removes his hands from his face to look up at Me. When he sees Me, his blood-shot eyes light up.

"R-rabbi? Rabbi Jesus? I-, is it really You?" he whimpers, sniffling and wiping his eyes and nose.

"Yes, My boy, I am Rabbi Jesus." I put My hand on the boy's back, patting it, soothingly. "Tell Me, why are you crying?"

"Well, Rabbi," the boy answers sullenly, "my friends and I came to see You, but some big, scary man stopped us and told us to go away. He said that You didn't have time to talk to us."

Hearing these heartbreaking words, I feel anger build up in My stomach. "Where, may I ask, is this big, scary man who told you this nonsense?"

"Over there, Sir, with eleven other men," the boy answers.

"Well, I am going to go reason with him."

I storm up to Simon and grab him by the collar. "Simon," I growl, "did you tell that little boy and his friends there to go away? That I did not have time for them?"

"Well ... I, I mean—" Simon stammers, taken aback.

"Do not say that! Do not *ever* say that!"

"But Lord, I figured You needed rest. I was only trying to help."

"If you want to help," I order, "then let the little children come to Me! Do not ever keep them from coming to Me! Do you not know that the kingdom of Heaven is only for those who would receive it like those little children do?"

Simon bows his head and replies, "Forgive me, Lord. I will let them come."

I smile and release My grip on him. "Good. Now let us go find them. They may still be nearby."

Sure enough, the boy is waiting for us in the exact same place where I had left him. With him are several other little boys and girls around his age, along with their parents. The oldest child among them is a young maiden who looks vaguely familiar to Me. She smiles when she sees Me and says, "Hello, Rabbi Jesus! Do You remember me?"

I am almost certain that I have met her before, but I do not wish to be wrong. I smile apologetically and cock My head.

"I was dead, but You came to my father's house and brought me back to life."

My eyes widen with joy and surprise. "Ah, yes! Now I remember! You are Jairus' little girl, aren't you?"

The girl nods excitedly. "Now I am fourteen years old and can help take care of the younger children in my village."

As the girl and I converse, Simon addresses the rest of the children and mutters his apology. "Er, I'm sorry for scaring you off, children. Please, call me Simon." He smiles sheepishly and extends his hand for the children to shake. The children eye his hand with caution and timidity before shaking it to show their pardon.

———

"And so the shepherd searched high and low for his lost lamb. Eventually, he heard the sound of desperate bleating in the distance. It was the sweetest sound he had ever heard in his life. He rushed over to the source of the sound and there, tangled up in a thorn-bush, was his precious little lamb."

"Was the shepherd angry with his lamb for wandering off?" one of the girls asks.

"Well, he rebuked it a little, but his anger was short-lived. Tears of joy and love filled his eyes, and he buried his face in the lamb's soiled fleece, kissing it."

"What did the shepherd do next?" a boy, sitting on My knee, asks excitedly.

"Well," I answer with a smile, "he joyously carried his little lamb home on his shoulders, of course. Upon reaching his home, he bathed it, dressed its wounds, and threw a great celebration for its safe return!"[31]

The children cheer and clap their hands at this wonderful, happy ending. I lift My eyes and see Jairus' daughter approaching Me with a bunch of large, white lilies in her hand.

"Here, Rabbi! I picked these for You!" she calls.

My eyes go wide as I behold both the beautiful gift and the adoration the girl has for Me. "Oh my," I gasp softly. "Ah, thank you, darling child. What a lovely surprise!"

For a while, I sit and admire the beauty of those lilies, My Father's gorgeous creation; the whiteness of their petals, like that of a lamb with the softness of a dove's feathers; their long, trumpeting necks and heads, resembling priestly shofars, reminding Me of My cousin's voice; even the fragrance of the flowers is sweet as the honey on My cousin's breath.

As I continue to breathe in the sweet yet increasingly powerful aroma, I feel a sudden irritation in My sinuses, and My nostrils begin to flare. I squeeze My eyes shut as My breath

---

[31] See The Parable of the Lost Sheep, found in Matthew 18:12–14 and Luke 15:3–7

catches in My throat. Finally, I bury My face in My elbow and turn away as an onslaught of sneezes overtakes Me.

Simon wanders over as My sneezing subsides. When he notices My pink-tinged nose and streaming eyes, his expression turns to one of alarm and concern. "Jesus," he asks softly, "are You all right?"

Perhaps he thinks that I started crying. I sniff and rub My nose with the back of My hand before giving My friend a reassuring smile. "Thank you for your concern, Simon, but I am quite all right. It is just these lilies My young friend here has given Me. I suppose I forgot how strong their fragrance was," I answer, massaging My throbbing forehead.

The young girl blushes in embarrassment and says quietly, "I am so sorry, Rabbi. I didn't know they would bother You so much. I can take them from You if You want."

"No, no, My child!" I exclaim with a soft laugh. Upon saying this, I take My satchel and gingerly place the delicate flowers in it. "See, they will be perfectly safe in there," I reassure Jairus' daughter, patting her on the shoulder. "Don't worry. They are a wonderful gift! I love them! More than that, though, I love *you!* All of you!"

Here, I usher the rest of the children to My side, "God, your Father in Heaven, loves you; every one of you. He loves you even more than the shepherd loves his lamb. Furthermore, He has created you for a very special purpose. I want you all to remember that and never let it go."

The younger children smile and nod, while the maiden's eyes fill with tears of joy and love as she whispers, "Yes, my Lord. I will remember."

———⁂———

That evening, as I am relaxing at My disciples' fire, Salome, the mother of James and John, the sons of Zebedee, comes to speak with Me.

"Lord," she begins, "I would like to ask a favor of You."

"All right, what would you like from Me?" I ask, genuinely interested in what the woman is going to ask.

"Well, I believe that You are the Messiah. You could be crowned King any day now. When You do, all I ask is that You allow my two sons to sit on either side of Your throne."

Shocked at her request, I answer, "Hmm. Well, I am not sure about that ..." Turning now to the two brothers, I ask, "Can you men drink from the cup that I am about to?"

The young men nod in affirmation, "Oh, most certainly, Lord!"

"And you shall," I reply, "but your request is not for Me to grant. It would be up to My Father."

Just then, My other ten disciples overhear our conversation.

"What?! You two?! The greatest in the Kingdom of heaven?! Just because your Abba[32] is richer than ours? What, is he going to *buy* you two your own thrones?" Simon sneers indignantly.

He smirks and takes his brother Andrew's arm. "Well, while we're on the subject, suppose the greatest position is reserved for the strongest? In that case, if anyone's going to be the greatest, it's going to be *my* brother and me!" The brothers flex their arm muscles to prove Simon's point.

"No, no, no," Judas chimes in. "Jesus would probably want people who are wise and good with money! Am I right, Matthew?" Matthew nods in agreement.

Hearing My disciples bicker and squabble like this, I sigh and pinch the bridge of My nose in vexation. *Will these men ever learn?*

To My relief, Thaddeus quietly murmurs, "Er, Jesus? What do *You* say? Who *will* be the greatest in Your Kingdom?"

---

[32] In Hebrew, the term "Abba" is a more affectionate equivalent of "Father." Simon is essentially calling James and John a couple of Daddy's Boys here. Also, it is believed that Zebedee was, in fact, financially better off than the other disciples' families were.

"Well, let Me show you," I answer, inviting the little boy I first met under the sycamore tree this morning to come join Me by the fire. He wanders over, and I take him in My arms.

"I can tell you one thing: unless you turn from your vain, selfish ways and become like this little child in My arms, you will not even make it through the *gate* of heaven." Noting the surprise and perplexity on My disciples' faces, I explain, "Whoever humbles themselves like this little child is the greatest in My Kingdom."

Just then, the other children, including Jairus' daughter, make their way over to our fire and gather around Me. I rise and spread My arms over their heads as I recite the Aaronic blessing:

"Children, may the Lord watch over you and bless you. May His face shine upon you. May the Lord set His countenance on you and grant you peace. Amen.[33]

---

[33] Numbers 6:24–26

CHAPTER 9

*"I am the Resurrection and the Life. He who believes in Me shall live,
even though he dies, and whoever lives and believes in Me will never die.
Do you believe this?"*
—*Jesus to Martha (John 11:25–26)*

——《》——

"**L**ord! Lord Jesus! Oh, where is He?"

The frantic messenger groans in perturbation before

twelve hands motion towards the stream. There, I am enter-

taining the children and teaching them how to skip stones

across the water. When I feel My disciples' eyes fixed on Me, I

turn to face My seeker.

The man calms down enough to articulate his words as he

declares, "I have come to deliver a message from your friends,

Mary and Martha."

I smile when I hear those dear women's names. *Ah, Mary
and Martha: Two women of very different elements. Martha, fiery
and big-boned, always wanting things to be perfect and in their
place within the household. Her sister Mary, on the other hand,
small and soft-spoken by comparison, enjoying every moment of*

every day, in every way she can. I remember the last time I visited their home like it was yesterday.

———◦◦◦———

There is a din and flurry of activity sounding from the kitchen as I enter the house. There is bread being baked, furniture being dusted, and wine being pressed. Martha does not even seem to notice My arrival and thus does not rise to greet Me. I feel surprised and a little hurt by this, but am glad when her sister gets up from her work, kisses Me, and leads Me to the best seat at the table. There, she asks Me questions about My travels and the wellbeing of My disciples. I answer her questions and converse with her, and soon we are laughing and basking in the mirth of each other's company.

Suddenly, I look up and see Martha standing in the doorway. Her hands are on her hips, hair disheveled, lips pursed into an angry scowl.

"Jesus!" she all but spits out My name, as if uttering a curse word. "Do You not care that my sister is out here at Your feet while I have been slaving away for hours this evening? Tell her to get up and help me this instant!"

No sooner have these words been spoken than Martha's bottom lip begins to quiver, and her eyes brim with bitter, exhausted tears that spill down her flour-dusted cheeks.

My heart shatters. Up until now, I have listened to the woman's complaint with calm patience, but when I watch her after she finishes, just standing there on the verge of collapsing on the floor and crying herself to sleep, it is more than I can take. I leap from my seat and pull her to Myself, kneading My hands through her shoulders, which are twisted up in knots from her labor.

"Martha, Martha," I purr into her ear. "Please, no more of this. You are so worried and upset by too many things at the moment. Only one thing matters, and you are experiencing it right here in My arms. Your sister has chosen this important matter. I will not take that from her, and neither should you."

Martha gives a deep, shuddering sigh as I brush the last of the tears from her face with My thumbs. "I am sorry, my Lord," she says hoarsely. "I love You so much, and I just want everything to be perfect for You."

"Ah, Martha, I know you do," I murmur with a gentle smile. "But now is the time to be still and rest in My presence. That is all I ask."

———◈———

My reminiscing is interrupted by the messenger's call: "Lord Jesus, Mary and Martha wanted me to deliver the message that the one You love is ill. They are begging You to come and lay Your hands on him. They believe that only You can save him so that he will not die."

The one I love? Who could that be? Then it occurs to Me: Lazarus! Mary and Martha's brother! My heart breaks for the family, and I rise to go. Just then, I feel My Father's hand press against My chest.

"Stop, My Son. Now is not the time. Wait two more days before You go."

"Two more days? But Father, by then, Lazarus might be—"

Then I make the connection. "Oh, of course, Father. You want Me to wait until Lazarus has passed. In this way, I may raise him from the dead to display Your glory and power to My disciples and the other mourners! Is that correct?"

My Father smiles and says, "Yes, that is exactly what I want You to do, My Son!"

"All right, Father, I will wait."

But then I hang My head at the thought of the grief, sorrow, and anger Mary and Martha will feel upon losing their brother. "But first, tell Me, Father, what am I to tell the messenger?"

"My Son, You are to simply speak the truth to him: that this sickness will not end in death. It is to bring glory to God and to the Son of God."

⸙

"It is time, My Son. Lazarus is dead. Round up Your disciples and be on Your way to Judea."

I do as I am told and begin rousing My disciples from their slumber.

"Up, My friends! It is time to return to Judea."

"Judea?" Thomas starts to object. "Didn't the people there try to shove You off a cliff once?"[34]

"Yes, Thomas, I remember well. But our friend Lazarus has fallen asleep. I need to go there to wake him up."

"Er, Jesus?" Judas asks, laughing incredulously. "Isn't sleeping the proper thing for Lazarus to be doing right now? Let the sick man get his rest so that he may get better."

I glance at Judas, My eyes stormy with sadness. "No, Judas. It is not that kind of sleep."

---

[34] See Luke 4:29

Judas' eyes go round with shock as he gasps, "You mean—"

"Yes," I answer plainly, "Lazarus is dead."

"What? Lazarus is dead?" Simon pushes Judas aside to put his arms around Me.

"Ahh, Jesus, we are sorry to hear that. How sad for Mary and Martha. How sad for *You*. First your cousin John and now—"

"Simon," I say with a slight smile, putting a hand on the bigger man's shoulder to calm him. "Do not pity Me. It was for all of your sakes that I did not go to heal him right away. In this way, you will believe in Me. I told you that I was going to go wake him up, did I not? Now, let us get moving!"

Thomas sighs and shrugs his shoulders. "Well, you heard the Man! Let's go to Judea. At least if they try to kill Him, they'll have to kill us too."

———

As My disciples and I head up the road towards the sisters' home, their messenger sees Me. I tell him to call for Martha and Mary. The man gives Me a piercing glare, but does as I have requested.

As I wait for the sisters, My heart aches with grief and anxiety. What will they think of Me? Will they try to chase Me away? Will they resent Me for not coming to their brother's aid in time?

At last, there is movement from the door, and Martha comes bounding out to meet Me, sobbing immensely. Through her sobs, she can only articulate the single phrase, "Jesus, why? Jesus, why?"

She continues this heart-wrenching phrase until she collapses into My waiting arms. Within moments, her words trail off, and all that remains are tears.

"Oh Martha, Martha. Shh, peace. I am here," I whisper in her ear as I rub circles on her heaving back.

After a while, Martha's sobs subside, and she is able to speak coherently, "Lord, if You had only been here sooner, my brother would not have died."

"Yes, Martha. I know."

"Oh, but Lord, I know that even now, God will do whatever You ask of Him."

A thrill of hope sparks through Me as I hear these words of faith. I turn and look Martha lovingly in the eye and proclaim, "Martha, Your brother will rise and live again. You know that, don't you?"

At this, Martha give Me a small, sad smile. "Yes Lord, I know. I know he will be resurrected at the end of time."

I smile back at her. "Martha, there is no need to wait until the end of time. The resurrection is not a *time;* in fact, it is not even an *it,* but a *He.* He is the One who is speaking to you this very moment. Martha, don't you see? *I* am the Resurrection and the Life. He who puts his trust in Me will live even after he dies, and whoever lives and believes in Me will never die. Do you believe these words that I am speaking to you?"

Martha's smile broadens as her red-rimmed eyes fill anew with tears. "Yes, Lord! I do believe! I believe that You are the promised Messiah!"

"Martha," I say, "go back inside and get Mary, your sister."

Martha nods and turns to go get Mary. After a few moments, the two of them return. Unlike Martha, Mary is not in a frenzy of emotion. She is more collected, only weeping quietly, like a cooing morning dove. This stark contrast to her sister only makes My heart ache afresh.

"Lord, why didn't You come sooner and save my brother?" she whimpers upon reaching Me. "I thought he was Your friend."

My voice trembles as I croak, "Show Me where your brother lies."

Mary and Martha take Me, one on each side, and walk Me up the road where their brother rests in his tomb. As we round the corner and I see the tomb, which has been sealed with a large, round stone, the anger and sorrow for the man's grieving sisters and the oppression of sin on the human race as a whole becomes too great for Me to bear, and I, too, begin to weep. Hot, bitter tears cascade down My cheeks, darkening the rocks and the dust of the road and like raindrops. I can feel the eyes of the other mourners fixed upon Me and hear their thoughts and murmurs:

"Ah, see how much Jesus loved Lazarus! Look how He weeps for him."

"If He really loved Lazarus, why did He let him die to begin with?"

By the time we reach Lazarus' tomb, I have regained My composure and brush the tears from My face.

"Now, take away the stone."

Martha grimaces and shakes her head. "Lord, by now there must be a terrible smell. He's been in there for four days now."[35]

I chuckle slightly at this comment before looking Martha in the eye and earnestly stating, "Martha, trust Me. I told you that if you believe, you shall see the glory of God."

---

[35] This number of days is significant in understanding Jesus' miracle. According to Jewish belief, the spirit of a person hung around the body up to three days after death. Therefore, with Jesus coming on the fourth day, all hope of a revival would have been demolished.

Martha blushes and bows her head. "Forgive my lack of faith, Lord. I will have the stone removed."

While some of the other mourners busy themselves with the removal of the stone, I turn to face the crowd and speak in a voice loud enough to be heard by all,

"I thank You, Father, because You have heard Me. I know that You always hear Me, but I say this for the people here in order that they may believe that You have sent Me."

After I have spoken the last word, I slip inside the tomb. "Lazarus," I command, raising My voice in authority, "come out!"

Issuing from the bundle of bandages comes a groan of exertion as the mummy-like body sits up. He swings his legs over the edge of the stone shelf he has been laying on for the last four days and slowly rises to his feet. I wrap My arms around him and carry him out from the grave, into the sunlight. As I remove the linen napkin from his head, my friend squints in pain from the brightness of the sun. Once his eyes are adjusted, they fall upon Me.

"Lord! Lord Jesus!" he exclaims groggily but happily. "Oh, my friend, You remembered me! I've been healed!"

Right after this joyous proclamation, the once dead man looks about a bit more and sees the large crowd of people watching him with white, alarmed faces, and his sisters looking on, tear streaks still visible on their cheeks.

"Er, what's happening? What's everyone looking at?" he inquiries, growing a bit embarrassed now.

"Er, Lazarus? Brother ..." Martha begins, a shaken and awe-struck expression on her face, hardly daring to believe what was happening. She motions behind Lazarus. The man's eyes widen as he slowly turns and sees the tomb from which he came out, with the stone rolled away from the entrance. His face goes red as he mumbles, "Have I been ... ?"

Mary, Martha, and I slowly nod.

After a few moments, My friend suddenly sees the humor in all this, and he throws his head back as hearty peals of laughter issue from his chest. Soon, his sisters and I are laughing with him. Mary and Martha, still in shock and great mirth, bolt towards Lazarus and hug and kiss him.

"All right, now take off all those wrappings and let the man walk freely," I instruct, trying to stop My laughter.

As soon as Lazarus is unwrapped and has bathed and clothed himself, Martha puts together supper for us all. Thus, what began as a sad and somber gathering of commiserates becomes an exuberant celebration as the people watch the once dead man sit at the table, eating, drinking, and laughing with his sisters and Me.

After we have eaten, Mary rises from her place and retreats to the kitchen. She returns bearing a precious, ornate jar of spikenard in her hands. With an ear-splitting crack that causes half the people in the room to jump, she breaks this precious jar and quickly holds it over My head. She works the fragrant oil into My hair with her fingers before she pours the rest of it over My sore and tired feet. Lastly, she stoops down and begins wiping the oil with her beautiful, long, dark hair. I tilt My head back and sigh as I breathe in the spicy-sweet aroma of the oil, a blissful yet somewhat melancholy wave washing over Me.

Across from Me, Judas' eyes flash in anger as he starts to protest, "A waste! A waste! That fine oil could have been sold! We could have fed thirty poor families with that money!"

"Shut up, you! Leave my sister alone!" Martha quips back in defense of Mary. "The Lord has just raised our brother from the dead. He deserves this beautiful gift." Apparently, the events of My last visit and everything that had taken place before supper has made her heart soften towards her sister.

"Martha is right, Judas. Do not deter Mary from her worship of Me," I rebuke. "The poor will always be in your midst; you can give to them whenever you please. Sadly, the same cannot be said about Me. That is why Mary has chosen to honor Me in this way. She is preparing My body for burial."

At My rebuke, Judas goes silent, but his eyes do not leave My face for a good half of a minute. His face holds an expression of what appears to be sullenness, but as I look back into his face, I believe that I see tears forming in his eyes, those gleaming green eyes that I had at first marveled at. Wait, it's coming back to Me now. I know where I had seen those eyes before. They are the same eyes that looked upon Me almost three years ago in the wilderness; the eyes that had set themselves on Me like a hungry lion's eyes, desiring to swallow Me up. I do not wish to dwell on the possibility, but I cannot help but wonder: *Could Judas Iscariot, one of My twelve chosen, be in league with the devil?*

CHAPTER 10

———

" **T**he time has come, My Son."

"Time?"

"Yes, time for the prophecy to be fulfilled. Time to win My people back to Me."

My Father's eyes grow sad now; much sadder than I have ever seen them before.

"Ah, Father, is this the time that I must die?"

My Father heaves a deep sigh and nods. "Yes, My Son. It is. Here is what to expect: You already know that the Pharisees and the teachers of the law will play a part in Your demise. They will have You arrested and handed over to the high priest. He, in turn, will hand You over to Pontius Pilate, the Roman governor, on false charges. Remember, I told You that one of Your very own will betray You to the Pharisees and the teachers of the law."

"One of My own? Who could it be?"

I gasp as the answer quickly occurs to Me: "Judas?!"

"Yes, My Son. Your friend and disciple, Judas Iscariot, will be the one to betray You to those who despise You. You see, Judas has grown increasingly disappointed in You. When You started Your ministry, he was under the illusion that You had come to deliver the people from the oppression of the Romans by way of conquest instead of from the oppression of sin and Satan by way of servitude. He has been deceived by Satan that by betraying You, he will be helping You prove Your rightful Kingship. Ultimately he will, but the way in which he will is going to be so terrible for You. And how terrible it will be for Judas when he realizes it. He will wish he had never been born."

Tears blur My vision as I think over My Father's prediction. *Judas? The last disciple I called to follow Me? The disciple whose eyes lit up at the first touch of My hand and who had always been so ready and eager to see My glory and power at work? Could he really be the one to betray Me?*

"Yes, poor Judas," I utter somberly.

My Father gives a small, comforting smile and says, "Oh, but Your other disciple, Peter, will fare much better. However, he too will falter. He will deny three times that he even knew You as You are standing trial. But after all this is over and You have risen from the dead, You shall restore him, and he shall go on to build Your church."

I ponder these next words a bit. *Peter? But I do not have a disciple by that name.*

Reading My thoughts, My Father corrects Me, replying, "Yes, You do. He was the very first of the twelve that You met."

"Oh, You mean Simon?"

"Yes, Simon. His name shall be called *Peter,* for on him, on that rock, You shall build Your church."

Simon. Peter. The man who has been My best friend and spokesperson from the very beginning. He will deny Me three times? This same man will start My church?

Later that morning, I gather My disciples to Me and ask them an important question:

"My friends, who do people say that I am?"

"Well, some say You are John the Baptist," answers Matthew.

"Others say You are Elijah," offers Nathanael.

"Still others say You are Jeremiah, Isaiah, or one of the other prophets," interjects Philip.

I smile and nod patiently before looking all of them in the eye and asking, "Ah, but what about *you?* Who do *you* say that I am?"

Without missing a beat, Simon, now Peter,[36] proudly declares, "I believe that You are the Christ, the Son of the living God."

My smile broadens as I clap Peter on the back. "Good for you, Simon! This truth could not have been revealed to you by ordinary men, but by God. Your name shall now be Peter, for on you, My rock, I shall establish My church!"

Slowly, My smile sinks into a frown of soberness as I softly yet earnestly say, "Now I must tell you all that it is time to return to Jerusalem."

Upon hearing this, Judas gives a cheer and pumps his fist up and down triumphantly. "Is this the time that You will finally receive Your throne and Kingdom?" he asks excitedly.

My heart sinks, and I heave a deep sigh before continuing, "Yes, Judas, but it will not be in the way you might imagine. In order to become King and receive My ultimate glory, I must die. I must be arrested, delivered up to the chief priests and

---

[36] From this point onward, Simon will be referred to as "Peter" or "Simon Peter."

teachers of the law, be tried and found guilty, and be killed. But I will rise to life again after three days. When I do, I will meet you back in Galilee."

As I look around, I see My disciples' facial expressions change from joyous anticipation to confused, chaotic, gloomy dread. Suddenly, Peter rises from his sitting position, grabs Me by the arm, and pulls Me aside.

"Lord, what are You talking about?!" he hisses. "You can't die! You can't let them kill You! You are so close! And what about *us?*! We've dropped *everything!* Our families, our livelihoods, *everything,* to follow You! And now that we are this close, You're telling us it was all for *nothing?*! Come off it, Man!"

You can't die ... You can't let them kill You ... Where have I heard these kinds of words before? Wait, I know!

"Get behind Me, Satan!" I hear Myself roar. "You are not thinking about the plans of God, but of the plans of man!"

No sooner have I shouted these words than I feel a twinge of guilt. I turn to look into Peter's eyes, but the bigger man shrinks and looks away like a little child who has just been scolded by an angry parent. He has his face covered, but I can tell that he is crying. I want to comfort him, but I instead turn, go back to the place I was when I was praying earlier, and lie down to recover from Peter's and My altercation.

⸎

That afternoon, I am woken up to the sound of My Father's voice.

"My Son, take three disciples with You and come with Me up the mountain of Zion. Two men will meet You there. They will introduce themselves to You and reveal more information about what will unfold during Your time in Jerusalem."

Immediately, I return to My disciples, who have also been sleeping, and eagerly whisper, "Peter?"

Peter is sitting among the other eleven, looking very forlorn.

"Peter!" I try again, more loudly this time.

He still doesn't look up.

Finally, I call aloud, "*Simon! Simon* Peter!"

Peter raises his head and when he sees Me, he flinches and tries to hide his face in his knees again. I reach out My hand and gently lift his bearded chin so that our eyes meet.

"Jesus," Peter begins, "I am sorry about earlier—"

"No, no," I speak quickly. "Do not worry about that now. In the meantime, arouse James and John. I would like to take you three on a retreat, just the four of us, on Mt. Zion."

Peter gives Me a quizzical look, but he gets up and nudges the sons of Zebedee. Within minutes, we are on our way up the hill.

———◈◈◈———

Our first night on the mountain, I repeat what I said to them before about what is going to happen to Me once I set foot in Jerusalem. Upon hearing My claims of death a second time, Peter hangs his head and quietly says, "Jesus, please don't be angry with me. But I just don't see why You would set Yourself up to die. You've done such wonderful things and shown us the way to life. How can You turn Your back on all of that now?"

In response, I sigh and touch Peter's shoulder.

"Peter, I love you; I love all of you. And I know that you love Me and do not want anything to befall Me. But this is part of My Father's plan. I Myself do not fully understand how or why I am to die. That is the reason I have brought you here with Me for a few days. My Father says that He will send two special messengers to Me who will explain things in more detail."

———◈◈◈———

For two days, the four of us fast and pray and sing hymns of praise. As the third day dawns, we are still asleep. I am the first to open My eyes, however, as the rising sun seems a hundred times its usual brightness. I shield My eyes and look down, only to find that the intense light is not coming from the sun, but from My own body! It is as though I am absorbing the radiance of the sun itself. But no, I am not absorbing the sun's light, but My Father's glory. I next notice something else: My clothes are pure and white; whiter than the fleece of a lamb and whiter than the feathers of a dove!

Just then, two men appear. The older of the two, a tall, broad-shouldered man with long, grey hair and beard, appears in front of Me. He has a wide smile on his wrinkled face and tears of joy shining in his eyes.

"Oh, I never thought I'd see this day," he gasps.

"Nor I," breathes a voice behind My back.

I turn My head to find the source of the second voice and I see ... John? My cousin John? Back from the dead with his head reattached to his body? There's that curly hair, that camel coat, and that springy, nimble body. But wait ... this man has darker hair and looks older than I remember. On his shoulders, there is perched not a pure, white dove, but a scraggly, black raven.[37]

Then I remember My manners.

---

[37] See 1 Kings 17:6

"Oh, excuse Me, Sir; I do not mean to stare. It is just that you remind Me so much of My cousin John, whom I have recently lost."

The man laughs and shakes his head. "It is quite all right, my Lord," he answers, "But no, I am not Your cousin John the Baptist. Rather, I am Elijah, the ancient prophet."

"Oh yes, and I am Moses, the lawgiver," the older man with the long gray beard interjects. "I suppose I should have introduced myself from the start," he adds with a sheepish grin. After taking a second glance at the man, I realize that the two stone tablets he holds underneath his arm should have given him away.

"Oh My ..." Now it is My turn to be in awe and wonder of these men. "Moses and Elijah! The law and the prophet!" Addressing Moses, I chuckle slightly and ask, "So Moses, you are finally in the Promised Land! How does that make you feel?"

Moses looks around a bit before shrugging dismissively and grunting, "Eh, it's all right, but it pales in comparison to the glories of Heaven!"

"That's right," Elijah says. "I myself was taken up in a flaming chariot! The finest chariots in all of Israel could never beat that."

I frown in perplexity now. "So, gentlemen, if you do not mind My asking, what *are* you doing here?"

At My inquiry, Moses gives a great, booming belly laugh reminiscent of My Father's as he claps Me on the back and answers, "Why, we came to speak with *You,* of course!"

"T-, to speak with *Me?*" I stammer before I remember My Father's words; with all the excitement that has overtaken Me, I have momentarily forgotten. "Oh, yes! That's right! You must be the two men My Father sent to speak with Me about My departure!"

"Yes, Jesus. That is exactly why we are here," Elijah answers, a hint of somberness etched on his face now.

He continues, "Interesting how I remind You of John the Baptist, Jesus. Because Your cousin actually based his preaching method off of my own. You might remember that I was the one who told the people to prepare the way of the Lord. I too dwelt along the banks of the Jordan. And I too angered a king who wished me dead."

"Yes, I remember your story well," I answer.

"Getting back to the subject at hand, do You remember the words spoken by John the Baptist when he saw You that day, approaching the river? The day You came to be baptized?"

"Why, yes! He called Me 'The Lamb of God who takes away the sin of the world.'"

"Well—"

"Ahem. Allow me, Elijah," Moses interrupts before directing his attention to Me.

"Now, Jesus, let us go back even further. Do You remember that day in the temple? The day You were twelve years old and attending Your first Passover?"

"Yes, Moses, I remember that day. My papa, My earthly papa I mean, gave Me a lamb, a spotless, innocent, frightened lamb, to take up the steps to the high priest. I remember feeling sorrowful and weeping for that lamb."

"You had a good reason for feeling that way, Jesus, and it was not just because You had a heart for animals. You had a heart for the people with the great responsibility of carrying out that sacrifice. Even at the early age of twelve, You knew, at least subconsciously, that there had to be another way to make atonement for sin. And God has made that other way."

I now go sober, lower My voice, and murmur, "It is Me, isn't it?"

Both Moses and Elijah bear grave, almost mournful, yet somewhat hopeful expressions and nod. Moses says, "Yes, my Lord. It is You. You are the sacrifice God, Your true Father, has sent; the final Passover Lamb for His people."

Suddenly, I remember something else from My temple experience. "So that is why God asked Father Abraham to sacrifice his son Isaac. It was a forerunner for God's own sacrifice of Me, *His* Son."

"Right You are, Jesus," Elijah replies. "My contemporaries wrote so many prophecies about You, Isaiah and Micah especially. Much of what was written about You regards Your death."

"And how *am* I to die?" I ask a little nervously yet courageously.

At My question, Moses swallows hard, his eyes going moist, and mutters one single, terrifying word: "Crucifixion."

My whole body freezes up. "What?" Perhaps I had heard him wrong.

"Crucifixion," Moses repeats. "For You see, Jesus, the Passover lambs are roasted on wooden spits over an open fire. Those Roman execution tools look exactly like giant spits. Everything You are is in accordance with the sacrificial system: You are obviously male; You are the first-born of Your parents; You have lived a perfect, sinless life, a life without blemish. The lambs' blood was to be spread on the doorposts and lintels of the Israelites' houses.[38] Your precious, innocent blood shall be spread on the doorposts of people's hearts. You are the ultimate

---

[38] See Exodus 12:6

Passover Lamb in every sense of the term. Therefore, there is no other way to atone for sin now except by Your crucifixion and death."

A chill runs down My back, and I begin shaking violently as these words and the truth of them penetrate My soul. Moses and Elijah wrap their arms around Me, and together we weep, silently at first, then progressively louder until—

"Er, Jesus? Why are You crying? Who are those men that You are speaking with?"

I look down and, through My tears, barely make out Peter yawning and rubbing his eyes. He blinks drowsily and darts his eyes here and there to locate the source of the two foreign voices. Eventually, his eyes fall upon the prophet and the law-giver, and he gives an excited yet terrified gasp.

"Moses and Elijah! The law and the prophet!"

Quickly, he rouses our two other friends and motions towards us.

"Lord," he exclaims turning back towards us, shielding his eyes from My brilliance. "This is incredible! It is awesome for us to be here right now! Say, aren't you gentlemen cold? If you'd like, I can set up three shelters[39] for the three of you!"

---

[39] Or booths. See Festival of Booths in Leviticus 23:33–44

I give My disciple a weak, shaky grin and turn to face My guests. "Peter, one of My disciples." The two men chuckle hoarsely and nod their heads in understanding.

Suddenly, a large, white cloud comes down from heaven, enveloping Moses, Elijah, and Me. A familiar voice speaks, addressing Peter, James, and John, "This is My beloved Son, whom I love. In Him, I am well pleased. Listen to Him."

After My Father has finished speaking, Moses and Elijah's eyes fill again with bittersweet tears, and they kiss Me on the cheeks as the cloud begins to rise. The last I see of them, they are bowing to Me as the cloud lifts them heavenward. I look down at My clothes and see that they are back to their original color and are no longer shining.

When I raise My eyes, I see Peter, James, and John facedown like dead men, only shaking. They must have collapsed out of shock and fear.

"Nothing to fear, My friends," I say gently, having regained composure. "My guests have departed. It is time we do as well." I take Peter's shoulders and hoist him up. I do the same with James and John.

"Oh, but before we go," I warn, "Do not mention anything about what you have seen until the Son of Man has returned to you from the dead."

CHAPTER 11

"Hosanna! Blessed is He who comes in the name of the Lord! Blessed is the coming kingdom of our father David! Hosanna in the highest!"
—Disciples and Jerusalem crowd (Mark 11:9–10)

"It is written, 'My house will be a house of prayer for all nations';
but you have made it 'a den of thieves!'"
—Jesus (Matthew 21:13)

———≈∾∾≈———

A s we descend the hill and meet up with the other nine disciples, I speak to Peter and John.

"Peter, John, before we enter Jerusalem, I would like you to go into Bethphage. There, you will find a donkey tied up with her young foal. Untie them and bring them to Me. I wish to ride the foal into the city."[40]

Overhearing My command, Judas scoffs and wrinkles his nose. "Ugh, Jesus," he grunts disgustedly, "Why choose some smelly, stubborn donkey, let alone a weak, wobbly little foal to

---

[40] To avoid confusion, Jesus would not have ridden both donkeys at the same time; He would have only ridden the foal. It is implied here that the mother donkey was present in order to give her foal some peace of mind, so that it would be calm enough to let Jesus ride it.

ride into victory? Wouldn't You rather ride a big, magnificent chariot pulled by a team of white horses?"

I smile gently and shake My head. "No, Judas, I want a foal. A chariot with white horses is suitable for a king coming to conquer. I do not. I am coming to establish peace and love and salvation. Do you not remember the words of Zechariah?[41] 'Rejoice greatly, O daughter of Zion! Shout, O daughter of Jerusalem! Behold, your King is coming to you; He is just and having salvation. Lowly and riding on a donkey. A foal, the foal of a donkey.'"[42]

"Lord, what do we say if the owners come out and ask us why we are taking their cattle?" Peter asks hesitantly.

"Just tell them that the Master needs them and you will bring them right back. The people will understand who you mean."

Peter and John nod in satisfaction and turn to go into the village.

After about fifteen minutes go by, the sound of frightened braying fills My ears. I look and see a young donkey with Peter and John struggling to drag him towards Me.

"Come on, little fellow! We need you to cooperate with us! Jesus needs to ride you into town," I hear Peter groan while

---

[41] Not to be confused with Zechariah, the father of John the Baptist.

[42] Zechariah 9:9

trying to maintain a sweet, comforting tone and making kissing noises with his lips.

"Peter, here. Let Me try to calm him," I offer.

Peter hands Me the rope tied to the skittish foal. I take the rope in one hand and place My other hand on top of the little foal's head, stroking his soft, velvety ears.

"There, there, little foal," I croon, still stroking his ears, looking deeply into his eyes. "Do not be afraid. I am not going to hurt you. My disciples are not going to hurt you. We just have a big day ahead of us, and I need you to cooperate right now. I need you to carry Me safely through the street on your back, up to about the steps of the temple. Can you do that for Me?"

After hearing My gentle words, the foal twitches an ear and bows his head in submission. Soon, John arrives, leading the full-grown donkey, the mother of the little foal, by her rope. I smile and stroke her soft nose before turning again to her foal. "Look, little foal. Your mama is going to Jerusalem, too. You will be safe with us."

Peter and John shrug off their outer cloaks and pile them onto the foal's back. After they do, I climb onto the pile of cloaks and sit down. Without making another fuss, the little foal begins clopping towards the city gate.

———❧———

We have not even entered the gate of Jerusalem when a large crowd of people gathers and flanks us on both sides. I watch as they shed their cloaks and lay them in the road, making a soft path for My foal's hooves. Many people even begin tearing off branches from nearby trees—mostly big, majestic palm branches, but also some small delicate olive branches, and even a few extra-leafy sycamore branches. From the lips of all the people, beginning with My disciples, come the words, "Hosanna! Blessed is the king who comes in the name of the Lord!"

As we enter the city, some pick branches up off the ground and begin waving them as they sing their song to Me. Some of the children reach out their little hands to pet the foal bearing Me on his back and even to shake My own hand. "Hosanna! Hosanna! Rabbi Jesus is our king!" they chant.

A part of Me is filled with gladness, but another part of Me is filled with deep, dark terror. I know that I enter this city with its worship and praise only to be despised and rejected five days later.

Suddenly, I hear other voices, but these are not voices of praise and adoration. They are voices of contempt and spite:

"Rabbi! Tell these people to be quiet! They are disturbing the peace!"

I dart My eyes in the direction of this complaint and see the chief priests and teachers of the law glaring at Me, arms crossed, with mean, ugly sneers on their faces.

"Why must I?" I answer. "Do you not know that even if every tongue were to be stilled, the very rocks and stones would cry out in worship?"

———✺———

I feel a wave of memories wash over Me as the glorious temple of Solomon comes into view. Suddenly, I am a small, knobby-kneed Boy of twelve again, only instead of My heart rejoicing and dancing with excitement upon beholding the city, it is weighted down by sorrow and pity. I am filled with the foreknowledge that this beautiful city will be destroyed by the Romans.

This thought weighs on Me and I lift My voice, wailing, "Oh, Jerusalem! Jerusalem! If only you, yes, even you, had known the very thing that would bring you peace! But now it is too late; these things are hidden from your hearts and minds. The days are coming when your enemies will set up a barricade around you, surrounding you and hemming you in on every side, and tear you down to the ground, you and your children with you. I tell you that they will not leave one stone upon another in you, because you did not know the time of your visitation."

After proclaiming this, I bury My face into the foal's mane and continue to weep. *Oh My beautiful city, destroyed! The pride of David. The pride of all My people, Israel. All destroyed within a matter of days. And to think that this all could have been avoided if she had only come to Me. I would have spread My arms over her and protected her like a hen guarding her chicks. But she did not want that. Now, it is too late.*

———◦◦◦———

By the time we approach the steps of the temple, I have finished My weeping, but there is still a numbness and emptiness in My soul. All I want to do is pray and feel near to My Father again. I am relieved when I step off the little foal and begin climbing the steps. My relief is cut short, however, when the sound that I hear is not the joyous sound of singing and worship, but the boisterous, clamoring uproar of cattle, twittering of birds, clanging of coins, and the muttering of the money-changers as they take money from foreign visitors, whose only wish is to partake in the Passover feast and festivities.

At this point, I am so angry and distraught, I feel I might be sick. Peter and John notice My agitated condition. "Master, are You all right?" Peter asks as he and the latter disciple put their arms around Mine, lest I collapse.

"No! I am *not* all right! Get off of Me!" I snarl as I break free from My disciples' grasp and dive headlong into the chaos.

First, I throw over the tables of the moneychangers, hearing the clatter and din of the denarii and talents as they fall to the stone floor like hailstones. "Get out of here, you!" I roar. "My Father's house is meant to be a house of prayer for *all* nations! But *you! You* have made it into a den of thieves!"

After this, I fashion a whip and begin driving the livestock out, hearing their despondent lowing and bleating as they stampede out. Finally, I seize the cages containing the sacrificial turtle-doves, shoving them at those selling them. "Get these out of here!" I bellow. "I will not let you make My Father's house into a marketplace!"[43] The moneychangers and those selling the animals for sacrifice cower at My rage and scramble out of the temple.

---

[43] Literary license: These were probably two different temple experiences; the first being the better-known story found in Matthew 21, the second found in John 2. These two accounts have been combined for clarity.

As the commotion dies down, I am still convulsing from the aftershock of My outbursts and slowly sink down against one of the pillars of My beloved Father's house, burying My face in My knees.

"Ah, Jesus. Master. What have You done?" John gasps in shock and pity as he stoops down and runs his fingers along My spine in a comforting manner.

"'My love for Your house burns in Me like a fire, and when others insult You, they insult Me as well,'" I rasp out, My words muffled by the folds of My robes. "The sixty-ninth Psalm, line nine."

—⁓⁓—

Eventually, the excitement desists completely, and the people move on with the activities of the day. Some rich folk come up the steps and begin pouring money into the treasury. The clanging and the clamor of their coins clashes in My ears, causing My head to throb. I groan in pain, grasp My head, and bury it deeper in My knees.

Suddenly, a new sound, a softer, much sweeter sound, presents itself. It is a soft *plip-plip* sound[44] like a spring rain. I

---

[44] The sound of two small, copper coins: mites

raise My head and see a poor widow dressed in tattered robes, bearing a soft, peaceful smile on her face.

Sighing in relief, I pick Myself off the ground and turn to My disciples. "Did you men see *that?*" I whisper in wonder and joy. I motion to the widow and explain to the Twelve, "I tell you the truth, that widow over there gave the most of all the people who gave today."

In response, My disciples look at one another and shake their heads in confusion.

"Don't you see?" I continue excitedly, "All of the others gave out of their wealth. They returned home possessing more money than they gave. But that widow gave out of her poverty. She has nothing left now. Nothing, that is, except the hope and trust that God will provide her with what she needs to live on for the rest of her life."

"Hmmm ..."

I hear Judas sneer before rubbing his hands together as if deep in thought. I look across from him and see the chief priests and teachers of the law gathering together and hear them grumbling and complaining against Me. As if on cue, Judas strides over to them; I already know what he is about to do.

———ᴑᴑ———

As the day draws to a close and Peter and John have left to return the two donkeys to their owners in Bethphage, I am exhausted and weary at heart. The disaster in the temple, the knowledge of the destruction of Jerusalem, and the constant reminder of My own doom weighs down heavily upon Me. However, as I turn to descend the steps and go My way, I hear a feeble voice call out.

"Jesus? Is that You? Was that You who was making all that commotion earlier?"

"Yes, my friend," another voice answers. "That's Jesus, all right."

I feel My face turn red from embarrassment. Are these people going to berate Me for what I have done? But when I turn to face My "accusers," all I see is a woman hobbling towards Me with a stick, a cloth around her eyes. I can tell that she is blind. Alongside her are two men with leprosy, soiled bandages shrouding every inch of their forms save for their eyes. Soon, another woman comes and motions to tell Me that she is deaf and mute.

"Jesus," the blind woman speaks again, "If that is indeed You, we want You to cure us, if You are willing."

In spite of Myself, I smile and answer, "Ah, My friends, of course I am willing!" With that, I begin laying My hands on them, beginning with the blind woman, and send them home whole. After seeing them off, I turn and find more of the ailing in their place. The more people I heal, the higher My spirit is lifted, as I hear the healed ones cry out in honest praise. *Yes! Some sanctity, purity!*

It is dark by the time I am finished. Despite feeling emotionally and physically drained, I have some joy and hope in My heart as I lay My head down for some much-needed but fitful sleep.

CHAPTER 12

"This is My body given for you; do this in memory of Me ...
This cup is the new covenant in My blood, which is poured out for you."
—Jesus (Luke 22:19–20)

"Do not let your hearts be troubled. You believe in God;
believe also in Me."
—Jesus (John 14:1)

———ⱄⱄ———

At last, on Thursday evening, we are gathered together
in the upper room of an inn for the Passover celebration.
I am glad for this because for the past three days, since the
incident in the temple, I have been feeling physically and emotionally uneasy. I haven't slept well all this time and haven't
been able to stomach much food or drink. I hope I will be able
to eat tonight.

While My disciples relax and kick off their sandals, I take
a cup of wine and try to see My reflection in its contents. I
look awful: There are dark shadows under My eyes from sleep
deprivation; My hair and beard are haggard and unkempt; My
robes bulge around My form from My decrease in weight. Even

though I'm only thirty-three years of age, I have the look and feel of a man thirty years older.

As the twelve start to wander towards the table, John stops and looks at Me. His eyes widen, then soften, as he sees My downtrodden countenance.

"Jesus?" he asks quietly. "Are You feeling all right? Have You been ill?"

I give him a weak, tired smile and say, "Peace, John. I shall explain everything later."

—⦿⦿⦿—

The evening goes on with My disciples eating, drinking, and carrying on with their conversations. I Myself can only pick and nibble away at My portion of lamb. After a while, I finally speak: "My friends, this is the last supper I share with you before it has found fulfillment."

As soon as I have spoken these words, the twelve go completely silent. No more words of conversation. No more sounds of feasting. No more sipping of wine. By now, everyone's plates are empty, or nearly empty, aside from My own. The women in charge of clearing and washing our dishes come out to collect our plates. The woman who takes Mine observes the uneaten heap of meat and gives Me a frown of concern.

I do not respond to this but slowly rise from My seat, remove My outer garment, and take a towel, girding My waist with it. Then I beckon My disciples to gather against the wall. Perplexed, they do as I say and creep over to the wall as I approach them with a basin of water.

Setting the basin down in front of John first, I clear My throat to get his attention. Looking abashed, John protrudes his feet out towards Me and I breathe in the ripe smell of dust, human sweat, and camel dung. I am not repulsed by the smell, but embrace it, for it is the smell of humanity, which I love and have come to cleanse and redeem. I reach out, take John's feet, and gently place them, one at a time, into the basin. I rub and massage his throbbing heels and soles before lifting his feet out of the water and drying them with the warm towel I had tied around My waist.

I begin to do the same for John's brother James and Peter's brother Andrew. However, as I am about to take Peter's ankle, Peter objects.

"Er, Jesus," he asks with uncertainty, "Are You really going to wash *my* feet too?"

I nod. "Peter, you do not understand what I am doing now, but you will understand later."

Suddenly, Peter jerks his foot away from Me at such a great force that a bit of the water sloshes out of the basin. "No, Lord," he shouts. "You shall *never* wash my feet! I won't let You!"

I sigh sadly as I look My disciple in the eye. "Peter, you must let Me wash your feet. If I do not wash them, you cannot have any part in Me."

Upon hearing My sobering words and seeing My earnest expression, Peter's whole attitude changes completely. "What? I can't? Jesus, of course I want a part in You! You're my best friend! Please forgive me," he pleads.

Here, he not only stretches his feet out towards Me, but also his neck and the palms of his hands. "Don't stop at my feet, Lord. Wash my hands and my head as well. Wash my everything!"

I chuckle softly at Peter's extreme change of attitude. "Ah, Peter. I do not need to wash all of you—just your feet," I say.

I now direct My attention to all of My disciples and say, "You see, those who have bathed are already clean. All of you are clean, except for one." I proceed to wash Peter's feet. In spite of himself, My friend grins and tries to hold back giggles as My fingers tickle his soles. After I have dried him off, I continue through the rest of My disciples. The last disciple I wash is Judas. He is the one I meant when I said, "All of you are clean, except for one."

Judas hasn't made eye contact with Me or given so much as a grunt upon greeting Me with the others before we arrived at the upper room. He had avoided Me all throughout supper. However, as I take his feet and drop them one at a time into the basin of water, he finally lifts his head to look at Me. When he does, I notice that My wayward disciple isn't looking so well himself. His face is a bit paler than usual, and his eyes are glazed over and red-rimmed as if he has been crying. He bears an expression that I cannot quite identify. Is it guilt? Is it pity? Resentfulness? I cannot tell.

I finish drying Judas' feet and lead My disciples back to the table.

—◈◈◈—

"Do any of you understand what I have just done?" I ask. When they shake their heads, I explain, "You men call Me 'Teacher' and 'Lord.' You are correct in doing so because that is who I am. Therefore, if I, your Lord and Teacher, can become your Servant and wash your feet, so must you also become servants and wash your brethren's feet." My disciples nod their heads in understanding and agreement. Each of them, that is, except for Judas, who seems to be trying to sink into the background.

Upon setting eyes on him, a deep, mournful sigh issues from My chest. It is so deep I feel My heart could break. Peter hears this and softly yet urgently asks, "Lord, whatever is the matter? Are You ill?"

I shake My head. "No Peter, I am not ill. I am very grieved, thinking about the news I must bear to you." At the sound of My tone, My disciples cock their heads in concern and focus their full attention on Me.

"This very night, one of you dining here is going to betray Me."

At this, everyone's eyes go wide and round as tombstones before a frantic frenzy arises, with all voices shouting at once:

"Lord, who could it be?!"

"Could it be *me?!*"

"Could it be *you?!*"

"*Me?!* I would *die* before I betrayed Jesus!"

"*I* would never betray You!"

"Surely it couldn't be *me*, Lord."

This last comment comes from the lips of the man who will indeed betray Me. Once the words leave his mouth, Judas realizes what he has said and buries his head in his arms onto the table as though trying again to disappear.

Meanwhile, John lays his own head on My chest and drapes his arm around My neck, both for comfort and in an attempt to comfort *Me*. Peter nudges him and whispers something in his ear. John nods at him then asks, "Lord, who *is* the man who is going to betray You?"

I close My eyes and heave another deep sigh. "My betrayer," I murmur, "will be the man who eats the bread that I dip into this bowl."

After speaking this, I take the loaf of bread before Me and dip a small piece of it into the bowl of bitter herbs.[45] The bracingly potent scent of chicory and horseradish fills My nostrils as I touch Judas' shoulder.

"Look, Jesus, I've told You. It's not me. It couldn't be."

"Yes, Judas. It *is* you. You have said it."

Discreetly, I slip the piece of bread dipped in the bitter herb mixture to my betrayer. He reluctantly receives it.

"Judas, whatever you need to do, do it quickly."

---

[45] The contents of this bowl are actually uncertain. It is commonly assumed that the Last Supper took place during the Passover Seder meal. If that is the case, the bitter herb mixture would have been in the bowl that Jesus dipped Judas' portion of bread into. See Exodus 12:8.

Judas slowly nods in submission and sniffles, his eyes going redder and moist, either from distress or from the pungency of the herbs or both. He swallows hard a couple of times before rising, turning on his heels, and staggering out the door. I look out the window and watch him slump down the road. The night has gone very dark. Dark as the eyes of his heart. Dark as My soul this evening.

After Judas' form has completely disappeared from My sight, I turn back to My remaining disciples and take the rest of the loaf of bread in My hands. I lift it above My head, bless it, and break it. I pass the two halves to Matthew on My left and John to My right.

"Take this and eat it," I command. "This is My body, freely given for you. Do this in memory of Me."

Once Matthew and John have finished passing the loaf around and everyone has eaten from it, I raise the cup of wine, bless it, and pass it around as well.

"Take this too and drink. This is My blood, poured out for the atonement of sins. Do this also in memory of Me."

"My children, it is time. I will not be with you much longer. I must go so that I may be glorified and the Father may be glorified through Me."

"But Lord," Peter asks forlornly, "Where *are* You going? Tell us!"

"Peter," I say, stroking his cheek, "where I am going, you cannot follow yet. But one day, you will."

"Lord," Peter croaks, on the verge of tears, "why *can't* I follow You now? I would literally go to prison, even lay my life down for You!"

Now, I remember the words My Father said to Me days ago.

"Would you *really* lay your life down for Me, Peter? The truth is, before the rooster crows twice tomorrow morning, you will have denied three times that you even *know* Me."

At this news, the tears that had been building up in Peter's eyes come flowing down his cheeks as he cries out, "No, Jesus! I *won't* deny You! I would *never* deny You! I've told You, You're my best Friend! Even if everyone else at this table, no, in the whole *world,* denies You, *I* never will!" The rest of My disciples nod their heads in agreement as tears fill their own eyes.

"My friends," I say, a small, soothing smile on My face, "do not let your hearts be troubled. You believe in God, My Father; now it is time to believe in Me as well. In My Father's house are many mansions. I need to go prepare a place for each and every one of you. If I go, I will come back and take you with Me. In this way, we will always be together."

Seeing My disciples calm down a little and smile at Me lifts My spirits slightly, and I suggest, "Now, how about we sing a hymn and go out to Gethsemane to pray?"

Hearing murmurs of approval, I lift My voice in song as the Eleven join in, some of their voices thick and garbled with emotion:

"When the Lord restored the fortunes of Zion,

we were like those who dreamed.

Our mouths were filled with laughter,

our tongues with songs of joy.

Then it was said among the nations,

'The Lord has done great things for them.'

The Lord has done great things for us,

and we are filled with joy.

Restore our fortunes, Lord,

like streams in the Negev.

Those who sow with tears

will reap with songs of joy.

Those who go out weeping

carrying seeds to sow,

will return with songs of joy,

carrying sheaves with them."[46]

---

[46] Psalm 26:1–6

CHAPTER 13

"Father, if You are willing, take this cup from Me;
yet not My will, but Yours be done."
—Jesus (Luke 22:42)

——◈◈◈——

While walking up the road leading to Gethsemane, I shiver as the cool early spring wind rustles through My hair. The breeze reminds Me of the late-night conversation I had with Nicodemus by the Jordan. I remember telling him that I would be like the snake in the wilderness, lifted up for all to look upon and be saved. Back then, I did not realize that this meant crucifixion, the slowest, most agonizing method of death, reserved for the most dastardly criminals.

Suddenly, approaching the garden, I lurch forward as if vomiting. My heart feels like it is made of lead and it begins beating at a rapid speed. I pull Peter, James, and John to My side and bid the rest of My disciples to sit.

"Ah, My friends," I groan, "My soul is overwhelmed with sorrow to the point of death. Stay here and keep watch while I pray."

I leave My other disciples, and Peter, James, John, and I begin our stroll through the olive groves until I find a good-sized stone to kneel down upon. Slowly, My knees buckle and fall onto the grass as I lift My head up to the opening in the treetops, My hands clasped onto the stone. When I do, I find that the stars have clustered into a constellation resembling the shape of a cup.

This horrifying image strikes more fear and agony into My soul as I cry out,

"Abba! Father! If it is Your will, please take this cup away from Me! I have been Yours since the beginning of time. I have been one with You. I never want to be separated from You, even for one day. In drinking this cup, this cup of lies, murder, heart-break, sin, and death, I fear it will mean Our separation. Father, I love You! I don't want this to happen. Oh, but Father, I want Your will to be done, not My own!"

This time, when I pray, My Father does not answer. I only see Him standing there in the heavens, holding this celestial cup in His hand.

———✦———

Suddenly, an overwhelming feeling of loneliness overtakes Me. It is as though I am the only living person on earth. Has something happened to My disciples?

Anxiously, I begin moving closer to the place where I last left My friends. The sight I behold is appalling and heartbreaking. There, curled up under the trees, are My disciples, some of them leaned up against each other, sound asleep. I notice that some of them have tearstains on their cheeks. They must still be grieving over what I said at supper.

I turn back to check on My three core disciples, in hopes that they, or at least Peter, were able to keep their eyes open and stay vigilant. But, no. They too have fallen asleep.

I want to weep, but I cannot. What I am witnessing goes far beyond tears. I instead watch silently, the intense loneliness swallowing Me whole. Finally, I trudge closer and rouse Peter.

"Simon Peter," I sigh heavily, "You said that I was your best friend. You said that you would even *die* for Me. Yet here, you cannot stay awake a single hour with Me."

Peter just looks at Me dumbly with sleep-clouded eyes, as if he has no idea what I am talking about. I sigh again and gently instruct the three men, "Stay awake and pray that you do not fall into temptation. I know that your spirits are willing. You *want* to stay awake. But your bodies are weary and weak. Pray for strength."

Receiving an exhausted nod, I creep back to My stone. There, My Father is waiting, still holding the dreaded cup, a stony, determined expression on His face. Upon seeing My Father this way, My heart palpitates even faster. My body temperature seems to rise dangerously, and soon, big drops of sweat pour down My face and pool inside the hollow of My collarbone.

"Father!" I pant, "Everything is possible with You! Is there truly no other way to redeem humankind? But if this cup cannot be taken away unless I drink it, then let Your will be done, not Mine! Father, You promised Me that if there was something You wanted Me to do, You would grant Me the strength to do it! I need this strength *now!*"

At My plea, My Father's expression changes and takes on that of pure love and grace. He reaches His left hand to the heavens, and when He lowers it again, I watch as a strong and mighty angel descends and lights upon the grass near the stone where I have been praying. After he has landed, I rise and walk over to meet him. He is broad-shouldered and tall with flowing, golden hair and eyes the color of clear river water. When he sees Me coming towards him, he takes Me in his arms and envelops Me in his wings.

Inside, I feel something like sparks shooting and surging through every vein in My body. After the feeling leaves, though I am in no less agony than before, I feel both emotionally and physically stronger than I have been. I bid My thanks to the angel and send him back to My Father.

"Father, thank You for hearing My prayer! I am ready now to carry out Your will! I promise You, Father, that I, Your true Word, will not return to You until I have accomplished what You desire! I will achieve the purpose for which You have sent Me![47] Your will be done!"

My Father nods, His expression both proud and mournful, His eyes laden with tears of inconsolable loss. He turns His face away and proceeds to pour the contents of His cup over My head. As I feel the first drop touch My flesh, I feel the same horrific heat and smell the same horrific stench that I had three years prior in the wilderness. I also hear thunder and cracks of lightning. Only this time, this agony, suffering, punishment, and separation from My Father *is* directed onto Me. I shudder

---

[47] See Isaiah 55:11

as I feel the emptiness of My soul, the knowledge of My Father's absence from Me.

However, I also have the knowledge of immense joy beyond all measure when I think that My death and separation from My Father will mean that the human race shall be brought back into communion with Him. Despite My grave pain, My heart rises with this knowledge of joy and I squeeze My eyes shut as I continue to pray harder than I have ever prayed before.

"Father, I pray that they will all be one, just as You and I are one- as You are in Me and I am in You. And may they be in Us so that the world will believe You sent Me. Father, I want these whom You have given Me to be with Me where I am. Then they can see all the glory You gave Me because You loved Me even before the world began![48]"

During My final prayer, I have felt Myself grow increasingly light-headed. Is it from My mind darting between knowledge of immense pain and knowledge of immense joy? Or is it from dehydration brought on by My profuse sweating? I suddenly feel a burst in My forehead, followed by a severe throbbing sensation.

---

[48] Literary license: Prayer of Jesus as recorded in John 17. It has been grouped with the better-known prayer recorded in Luke for clarity.

I open My eyes to find drops of deep red sprinkled onto My stone. Cautiously, I put My fingers to My face, only to bring them out sticky and red: Blood. I must have erupted some veins from praying so fervently.

By now, Judas and the temple officers must be on their way to arrest Me. I need to prepare My disciples and Myself to go out and greet them. I begin trekking back to them, only to find them still dozing the night away.

"What?" I whisper, "Are you men *still* sleeping?"

Just then, I see dots of light coming closer towards us. Judas and his crew are fast approaching. There is no time to express My hurt and loneliness now. I sigh and speak loudly enough to awaken My slumbering disciples.

"Well, you might as well get up now. The hour has come for the Son of Man to be betrayed."

Upon hearing My words, My disciples somehow find their strength and they spring to their feet, as if prepared to fight. Meanwhile, in the distance, I can just make out the words Judas is speaking to Caiaphas' servant, Malchus.

"The Man I kiss is the Man you want. When I give the signal, seize Him!"

In an instant, Judas practically slithers up next to Me and feigns a friendly tone as he says, "Greetings, Rabbi." His rough, un-groomed stubble chafes Me, and I smell the bitter herbs on his breath as he grabs Me by the collar and plants a kiss on My cheek.

"My friend," I say in a voice barely above a whisper, "do whatever you came here for. But do it quickly, for it is with a kiss that you betray the Son of Man."

My wayward disciple hesitates only for a moment before motioning to Malchus and the others, who charge out of the groves, armed with swords and clubs. Before they come too close to my disciples and Me, however, I ask firmly, "You there, who is it you want?"

"Jesus of Nazareth," they answer gruffly.

"I am He," I answer plainly.

These three words seem to momentarily disarm My pursuers as they fall back onto the ground as if in shock.

"What are you doing on the ground? Get up and tell Me who you want!" I command.

The soldiers scramble to their feet and reply, a bit shaken this time, "We've told You: Jesus of Nazareth."

"And I have told you: I am He," I answer. "Therefore, if it is just Me that you want, let the other men go."

No sooner has the last word left My lips than Peter's eyes flash with anger.

"You there," he barks. "Don't even try to take Jesus away! I'm warning you! I'm well-armed!"

With a mighty swing of his sword, he slashes the high priest's servant's ear clean off as one would a young sprout. Blood and chunks of flesh spew in every direction as Malchus doubles over, wincing and moaning in pain. *Malchus. You have shed your blood in order to deliver Me up to your master, Caiaphas. But tomorrow, I shall shed My own blood in order to deliver you to My Father. You and all humankind.*

"Stop!" I shout. "No more of this!" It is My mission to restore order back to My Father's creation, and for three years, I have done just that. I will not stop, even now.

I stoop down and pick up the bloody appendage. "Peace, Malchus. Be made whole." With that, I press the ear to the hole on the side of Malchus' head, which is still gushing blood. When I do, immediately, the ear clamps down and is made whole without so much as a scar. In fact, there is not a sign of injury anywhere, as if Peter's sword had never struck. Malchus gasps in stunned surprise before sighing in relief.

"Now then," I say, upon seeing that Malchus is restored, "why have you gone through the fuss of coming at Me with clubs and swords as if I were a common criminal? I have been teaching in the temple day after day; you could have arrested Me at any time during those hours."

I then turn My attention to Peter. *Ah, Peter, someday soon, you'll understand.*

"As for *you*, Peter," I sternly rebuke, "do you not think that My Father could send Me twelve legions of angels to My rescue if I asked? But then, how would the scriptures be fulfilled?"

Peter says nothing but gives Me a look of both sullenness and apprehension.

Malchus, meanwhile finding his voice, clears his throat and mutters, "Er, th-, thank You, Rabbi. I—"[49]

"No, no, go ahead. Just take Me quickly," I answer reassuringly.

Malchus sighs in pity and motions for the other officers to take Me by My arms. They seize Me and begin to take Me away. In sorrow, I turn My head to look behind Me. One of the officers

---

[49] Creative license: Malchus' response to being healed is unknown. However, some believe that he was grateful to and ultimately ended up believing in Jesus, as he is the only one of the officers who is called by name.

gives Me a kick to tell Me to keep moving, but I have already seen My disciples shake and run for their homes as quickly as their legs can carry them.

But wait: Where are Peter and John going?

CHAPTER 14

"I am (the Christ). And you will see the Son of Man sitting at the right hand of the Mighty One and coming on the clouds of heaven."
—Jesus to Caiaphas (Mark 14:62)

"What shall I do, then, with Jesus who is called the Messiah?"
"Crucify him!"
—Pontius Pilate and the crowd (Matthew 27:22)

———

T he cords fastening My arms are so tight that they cut into My flesh as My captors push Me along to the palace of the former high priest, Annas. My face burns red and hot from the humiliation of being taken prisoner and subjected to the mercy of these angry Temple officers. I know that I have all authority on earth to free Myself from their grasp and run, but I cannot; the prize and the reward are too great for Me to forfeit.

When Annas lays eyes on Me, he gazes for a few moments before narrowing his eyes in utter contempt. I stare back at him. It was he who I ruined financially by clearing the Temple and scattering the moneychangers' coins last Sunday.

"So, Jesus," Annas begins, "what brings You to my palace tonight? I hear many stories about Your disciples and what You have been teaching them. Is it true that You have recently spoken against paying taxes to the emperor?"

Annas continues, question after question; questions that I know to be illegal. Eventually, I answer with a question of My own:

"Why must you question *Me?* Why not ask those who have listened to My words? After all, I have always spoken publicly in the synagogues and temple where all the Jews gather. Ask *them.*"

No sooner have these words been spoken than I feel a sudden sting of an officer's palm slapping Me across the face.

"Is that any way to answer the high priest?"[50] he hisses.

I stagger a bit in shock and pain before turning to My attacker and asking firmly, "Why? Why have you hit Me? If I have said something wrong, tell Me what I said. If I have stated the truth, why do you strike Me?"

I look back at Annas, who bears neither a smile of approval nor a frown of disapproval.[51] His face is simply etched with vexation and disinterest. Finally, he waves his hand flippantly and

---

[50] Not the present high priest. Annas was high priest before the Romans took over Jerusalem. Now, his son-in-law, Caiaphas, is high priest.

[51] The officer's brutal act of slapping Jesus would have also been illegal.

announces, "Well, gentlemen, I am not getting anywhere with this Jesus. Send Him to my son-in-law, Caiaphas. I know he's got actual witnesses to attest to this man's words and crimes."

——⫷⫸——

The guards nod and yank Me by the cords to order Me to get moving. I do so, but not before hearing these fateful words:

"Liars! Liars and fools, the lot of you! I don't know the man! May God curse me if I do! Now, let me be!"

As Peter turns his head, I instantly hear the *Kee-kee-ree-koo! Kee-kee-ree-koo!* of a rooster, and Peter finds himself face-to-face with Me. My eyes go soft with both hurt and love. *Simon, Simon, I had told you at supper that this would happen; that Satan would try to sift you like flour and scatter you to the wind. But I will come back to you and restore you. After I have restored you, you shall restore your brethren.*[52]

Upon seeing the love and hurt in My eyes, Peter goes white in horror of what he had just said before fleeing out of the courtyard, crying harder than I have ever heard him cry before. A couple moments later, John comes hurrying out behind him, wondering what's gone wrong.

---

[52] Jesus actually spoke these words to Peter at the Last Supper when He predicted Peter's denial to him.

By now, Caiaphas is ready for Me. As My second trial commences, however, I notice inconsistencies in the "witnesses." For example, two witnesses come forward, and one says, "We heard this fellow say, 'I will destroy the temple and build it back up in three days!'"

The second witness shakes his head and argues, "No, no, no! He merely said, 'I have the *power to* destroy the temple.'"

Fed up with the inconsistencies, Caiaphas asks Me directly, "Well, don't You hear these charges made against You? What do You have to say for Yourself?"

I remain silent and continue to look around the room at all of the angry, hate-filled faces staring back at Me.

Caiaphas sighs impatiently and says, "All right, here is my final question that You *must* answer: Are You the Messiah, the Son of the Blessed One?"

Feeling a rush of courage, I stand up straighter and taller and confidently proclaim, "I am." I watch as the high priest's face goes from ashen to nearly blood-red as I go on, "And you shall see the Son of Man seated at the place of power at the right hand of God, coming on the clouds of heaven."

As the last words of My answer reverberate off the palace walls, Caiaphas begins shaking violently, and he tears his robes, screaming, "Argh! Why bring in any more witnesses?! You have all heard what this fellow has said! He is a blasphemer! What is your verdict?"

The vote is unanimous: "Guilty! He deserves to die!"

The next thing I know, I am blindfolded and feel big, strong fists striking Me in the face every which way. I hear the officers laugh and taunt, "Prophecy to us, Christ: Who hit You? Who's going to hit You next? Ha-ha-ha!"

After a while, they get tired of their game, tear the blindfold from My eyes, and begin dragging Me to the prison in Caiaphas' dungeon.

For two long hours, I sit in darkness, coughing occasionally as I breathe in dust and the filthy stench of human sweat and foul waste. Despite My exhaustion, I cannot fall asleep, both because of the stench and because of My cellmate's nasally snoring. His hair is dirty and matted, his teeth yellow and worn down. However, he seems physically fit, perhaps from many years spent on the run and participating in street brawls.

Just as I am about to close My eyes to rest them, the prison door creaks open and a hand reaches in to snatch Me up.

"Time for Your third trial, *Messiah*," a gruff voice sneers. I adjust My vision to the light and see the Temple officers, who grab Me and begin shoving Me back in front of the council where all of the religious leaders, including the high priest, the scribes, and the whole Sanhedrin, are waiting for Me, bearing sadistic smiles. I inwardly sigh in relief that out of all these dirty, sanctimonious faces, neither Nicodemus nor Joseph of Arimathea[53] is one of them. May God bless them and count their vote on behalf of Me to their glory forever!

"All right, gentlemen, we have found this man, Jesus of Nazareth, guilty of all charges. Sadly, we in Jerusalem have no law or right to condemn this man to death. Therefore, we must send Him to Pilate—"

"Wait!"

A familiar voice cries out in protest. In shock, Caiaphas turns toward the source of the frantic voice.

"Judas Iscariot?" he asks in both annoyance and shock. "Why do you interrupt our ongoing trial?"

Judas' voice goes quiet yet urgent: "I have made a terrible mistake. I would ask that you take your money back and let my master go free! I now realize that He is an innocent man and I

---

[53] Another member of the Pharisaic party and disciple of Christ, though not one of the original Twelve

have betrayed His blood. Please take your money back and give me back my master!"

"Innocent man? Ha! What is that to us now? You've already made your decision; now you must deal with the consequences yourself."

My betrayer's face falls for a moment before scrunching up in anger and going red. In a fury, he flicks his wrist and flings the bag containing the thirty silver pieces, the clashing noise of the coins ringing in My ears. I turn to look at him.

"Judas, peace. Be still."

"No, Lord! I cannot!" Judas snaps before whining, "Oh, Jesus, why didn't You escape when You had the chance?" Without another word, Judas breaks down bawling before turning and dashing out of the court, down the steps, and into the darkness. This is the last I will ever see of him.

—⁂—

"What charges are you bringing against this man?" the Roman governor, Pilate, asks. He then gives a yawn of both annoyance and fatigue at having been woken up to try Me.[54]

---

[54] It would have probably been five in the morning by this point. The religious leaders could not have gone into the house of a non-Jew to have Jesus tried, as that would have made them ritually unclean and unfit to participate in the Passover feast. Therefore, Pilate had to come out to meet *them*.

The Jewish leaders cock their heads at Pilate incredulously and mutter, "Do you think we would have brought Him to you if He was not guilty of a crime? We have found Him guilty of subversion, opposing paying taxes to Caesar, and claiming to be king of the Jews. He is a threat to our city and a threat to Rome!"

Pilate sighs wearily before pulling Me aside to interrogate Me in private. His expression is soft, almost one of pity and awe.

"*Are* You the king of the Jews?"

I cock My head at him and again answer with another question: "Is this your own question, or are you asking for others?" In this way, I search and observe the governor's own conscience.

At My question, Pilate gives a disgusted face before scoffing, "What? Am I a Jew? Listen, Your own people and chief priests have handed You over to me. Surely, You must know why?"

I look Pilate in the eye and stoically state, "My Kingdom is not of *this* world. Do you not think that My servants would have fought to prevent My arrest if it were? No, My Kingdom is of another place."

The corners of Pilate's mouth turn up in triumph at finally getting answers, and he half asks, half exclaims, "Aha! So You *are* a king then?"

I reply, "So you have said. Actually, I was born and came into this world to testify to the Truth. Everyone on this side of the Truth listens to Me."

At this, the governor's face falls and he bemoans, "Ah, but what *is* Truth?" For a few long moments, he sits, massaging his forehead before clearing his throat, turning to the crowd of religious leaders, and reporting, "I find no charge against this man. Besides, He is a Galilean rebel. Go whine your case to Herod, not to me."

———〜〜〜———

"Jesus? Oh my, You've come at last!"

The Jewish monarch smiles from ear to ear as he rises to meet Me. "I have heard so much about You! At first, I mistook You for Your poor friend, John the Baptist. The wife just woke up one morning, and his head was nowhere to be found![55] Such a shame what happened to him, really."

I make no reply but let My eyes wander around the throne room. Surprised by My silence and vacant expression, Herod nervously chuckles, "Er, I was hoping that since You are here,

---

[55] See Matthew 14:2. According to Catholic tradition, the disciples snuck into the yard outside Herod's palace and stole John the Baptist's head in order to give it a proper burial. This might explain why the king thought that Jesus was John the Baptist resurrected.

You could show us a few of these tricks You have been performing lately. Hmm, let's see ... Walk across my bathing pool? Perhaps divide these grapes and cheese between my servants and me? Do whatever You want."

When I continue to ignore Herod's words, the Roman guards grin vehemently and snarl, "Ha, we knew it! This man is not the Christ! He is a fraud!"

Upon hearing their accusations, Herod's face twists into a smile of contempt and false piety.

"Now, now, gentlemen," he says slowly and dangerously, "I assure you that our friend Jesus here is just a little timid and uptight at the moment. Perhaps He would feel better if given the proper attire." He claps his hands and one of the guards brings out a beautiful, deep purple robe. As they dress Me in it, however, I realize that this is not soft, fine silk, but a rough, crude material that scratches each time I move.

"Say, Jesus," Herod smirks, his smile growing uglier and meaner with every syllable, "would You like a *crown* to go with that royal robe?" Another guard comes, carefully bearing not a precious, golden crown with priceless, glittering jewels, but a hideous wreath of sharp thorns. I wince and writhe in pain as he jams it over My already aching head, its thorns slicing My scalp. I shut My eyes as the warm blood dribbles down My face like red tears. Then they reach for a makeshift scepter, really a whittled branch, and force it into My hand.

"All hail King of the Jews! All hail King of the Jews!" the Romans all cheer in mock reverence.

"O, Great One, Most Excellent! What is Your decree?" they jeer, bowing. "Shall we kiss Your feet?" They pucker up their lips to pretend to kiss Me, only to inhale sharply and spit in My face. Lastly, they take the stick from My hand and beat Me over the head with it again and again.

Meanwhile, I know that I do not have to go through all of this. I could escape at any moment, even now. At the very least, I could spit back, argue back, fight back. But, like a sheep at its sheerer, I do not open My mouth.[56]

Finally, Herod feigns a bored expression and grumbles, "All right, all right, let's get back to business, shall we? Send this *king* back to Pilate and let Rome decide what is to be done. Oh, and tell him that his dear friend Herod says 'Hello.'"

*So, Herod and Pilate are about to become friends because of Me. Is My prayer for unity slowly coming to fruition? Oh, but it is for the wrong cause: The duo is coming together **against***

---

[56] See Isaiah 53:7–8

*Me. Blessed are those who come together instead **in** Me and in My name.*

⎯⎯∞∞∞⎯⎯

Upon setting eyes on My bloody, spat-upon face, Pilate gasps in shock. "By the gods, Jesus! What have they done to You?"

Turning to the Roman guards now, he asks, "Why have you brought this man back to me? What did Herod have to say?"

One of the guards shrugs and mumbles, "Besides stubborn non-response, there is no charge from Herod against Him, either." He adds, "Oh, and the king sends his warm regards."

Pilate gives a surprised and flattered smile at this last remark before a messenger charges into the room, calling, "Pilate! Pilate! Your wife! She has sent you an urgent message! You must read it right away!"

Reluctantly, Pilate takes the scroll from the messenger and reads,

"My husband, please do not have anything to do with this Jesus of Nazareth! I am begging you! Last night, I had a frightening dream concerning Him! He is an innocent man! A good man! You know He is! Please, just leave Him alone!"

Pilate sighs as he rolls the scroll back up and hands it back to the messenger. "Woman's hysterical these days," he mutters.

Then, the governor's eyes and mouth simultaneously widen as if he had just formed a brilliant idea. He whispers something into the ear of one of the guards and sends him to the prisons. After about ten minutes, the man returns, dragging along the same broken man I had shared a cell with just a few hours ago.

"Now, Jesus," Pilate declares triumphantly, "this is Barabbas. Barabbas here has been held in prison on a count of murder and instigating a rebellion against my people. Since it is Passover, the people are going to decide who gets to go free and who gets sentenced to Calvary. Who do You suppose the people are going to ask to be released: You or Barabbas?"

Once again, I say nothing. Pilate raises an eyebrow and frowns in wonder at My unresponsiveness. At last, he shrugs his shoulders and orders, "Well, all right. Both of you in your positions on the platform! The crowd is waiting."

———⟊⟊⟊———

Sure enough, as Barabbas and I shuffle out onto the platform, we are greeted by a wild and angry mob of people. Before I can make out the words they are speaking, I hear Pilate's loud, booming voice call out,

"All right, people! I understand that you Jews hold a tradition of releasing one prisoner of your choosing at Passover.

In observation of this tradition, here I have these prisoners: Barabbas, a convicted murderer and insurrectionist against Rome, and a Man they call 'Jesus of Nazareth, the King of the Jews.' Who do you want?"

From the corner of My eye, I see the Pharisees stirring up the crowd and mumbling to them. Soon, I hear a cry from out of the crowd:

"We want Barabbas!"

"Yes, Barabbas!"

"Give us Barabbas!"

Upon hearing this unexpected, undesired answer, Pilate breaks into a sweat, and his mouth goes round. "Oh ... er ... but don't you want your king?"

Caiaphas turns to Pilate, bears his teeth at him, and hisses, "The only king we want is Caesar. Therefore, if you let this man, this blasphemer, go free, you are no longer a friend of Caesar's."

"Yes, but what *am* I to do with this man, Jesus the King of the Jews?

Immediately, the crowd roars, "Crucify Him! Crucify Him!"

"Ah, but *why?*" Pilate nearly whines out, "What crime has He committed against you? I've found *nothing!*"

"Crucify Him! Crucify Him!" the people yell even louder.

Pilate gives a wince before grabbing a guard and ducking back into his courtyard. "All right, new plan: let's flog Him. Hopefully, seeing His blood shed will satisfy these vultures."

Before I can process another thought, two Roman guards grab Me and drag Me to the whipping post. As they chain Me up, My knees start knocking together. All the slaps, punches, even the crown of thorns upon My brow, do not compare to the pain of being struck by one of these cat-o-nine-tails.[57] As one of the Romans lifts up My robes, he flashes the whip before My eyes. Once again, the temptation to flee or at least bat the torture instruments out of the Romans' hands is strong, but My intense faithfulness to My Father and My love of the human race give Me the strength to stay as the fist holding the first whip winds up and lashes it against the exposed skin of My back.

I howl in pain and hiss through My teeth as the guards rip the end of their whips out from My now flayed flesh and wind up a second time. As the flogging continues, I peer back occasionally to see blood spewing out, staining the bricks of the courtyard with gore, as well as big, long strips of My skin hanging out from

---

[57] One type of flogging torture instrument commonly used to inflict punishment on prisoners before their deaths; a whip studded with sharp pieces of metal or bone that would violently tear the prisoner's skin. Traditionally, they would inflict forty lashes minus one, as the fortieth lash is thought to altogether kill the prisoner, due to immense blood loss.

My back. All the while, I am still screaming and groaning in pain. Eventually I feel My shoulders, back, and calves throb and ache as their veins are now being struck, pouring forth even more blood. At this point, My system can no longer stomach the pain and the horrible sight; I double over and vomit onto My post.

The guards see this, and they laugh and congratulate each other before continuing their vile treatment. However, just as they are about to strike Me again, Pilate comes back and raises his hand.

"All right, enough, men! Let's try this one more time and see if the people are satisfied and agree to let Him go."

The guards nod and drag Me away. All the while, I hiccough and wince anew in pain as the rocks and gravel braze My now shredded body.

—⁂—

"Look, here is your man," Pilate announces to the crowd. Upon setting eyes on Me, the chief priests and teachers of the law again bear their teeth and howl, "Crucify Him! Crucify Him!"

"Why drag me into all of this? Can't you Jews crucify Him yourselves?"

"We've told you before that we don't have the right to put a man to death. But this man claims to be the Son of God. In our laws, that is blasphemy!"

A gasp of pain escapes My lungs as the governor seizes My lacerated shoulder and pulls Me into his courtroom.

"Where do You come from, Jesus?" he asks, tears of desperation forming in his eyes. Upon receiving silence as My answer, he whimpers, "Why do you insist on remaining silent? Don't You understand what is at stake here? That I am the only one at this moment with the power to free You or to execute You?"

Finally, I give him a verbal reply. I croak out through a dry and raspy throat, "You would have no power over Me at all unless it were given you from above. The ones who delivered Me up to you have the greater sin."

Again exiting the courtroom and facing the crowd, Pilate pleads one final time, "People, I implore you! Take your king and go your way!"

Caiaphas narrows his eyes in anger and growls, "Once again, we have no king but Caesar!"

All the people behind the high priest cry out in agreement, "Away with this man! Crucify Him!"

After a few more moments of listening to the crowd's angry shouting, Pilate goes crimson, and he bellows, "You know what?! Fine! I *will* have this man crucified! Guards, bring me my water basin!" The guards do so and Pilate plunges his hands into the water and scrubs in a vain attempt to wash himself of the responsibility of My death as he mutters, "I am innocent of this man's blood. The responsibility is yours!"

The look on the religious leaders' faces is that of sheer delight as the people cheer, "Yes! Yes! May His blood be on us and on our children!"

Oh, if they only knew what the words they are saying will come to mean!

CHAPTER 15

"Father, forgive them, for they know not what they do."
—Jesus (Luke 23:34)

"Father, into Your hands I commend My spirit."
—Jesus (Luke 23:46)

———✺———

The Roman guards rip the scratchy scarlet robe off My back, and I scream in pain as it adheres and peels from the areas where My skin had been torn from the scourging. Once I am back in My own clothes and watch the blood from the backside of My body soak into the linen, the guards drop a three-hundred-pound wooden cross onto My shoulders and grunt, pointing up the road leading to Calvary's hill, Golgotha. Straining My eyes, I make out the face of a skull in the indents of the cliffs, a symbol of My certain death.

"All right, get going, You!"

One of the Roman guards kicks Me in the shins and laughs maliciously as I fall, seemingly crushed under the weight of My cross. With a groan, I arise halfway and start staggering up the road. A multitude of people have come out to watch the spectacle. Many are those who were at My last trial. I hear their mocking voices:

"Ha! The fellow claims to raise the dead, yet He can't even lift His own cross!"

"Some king *He* would have made!"

However, other people, the ones who love Me, have also come, just to see if the rumors were true that I had indeed been sentenced to death. Most of these are women of the city including Suzanne, Johanna, Mary Magdalene, and My own mother. Their faces are white with shock and grief; they can articulate no words; they just stand there, weeping and wailing for Me.

Despite My excruciating pain, My heart aches for them and I hobble towards them, bearing the weakest semblance of a smile. "Oh, My daughters," I whisper, "Oh My dearest daughters of Jerusalem. Do not weep for Me; weep for yourselves and your children as well. For the time will come when you will say, 'Blessed are the childless women, the wombs that never bore and the breasts that never nursed.' Then, the people will say to the mountains, 'Fall on us!' and to the hills, 'Cover us!' For if people do these things when the tree is green, what will happen when it is dry?"

Not two moments after I had finished speaking, I feel another hard kick from one of My guards and I fall to the road, earning another wailing cry from My friends.

The second guard behind Me shakes his head in disapproval and mutters to the one who kicked Me, "Kicking this man is not going to get us anywhere. He is simply too weak and battered to carry a whole cross up the hill on His own. And we need Him dead by sundown. What else could we do?"

The two Romans search the crowd. Finally, they call out, "You there! Simon the Cyrene!"

The man in question timidly comes forward. He is an older man than I; however, he is strong-looking, with bulky arm muscles.

"Yes, you! You look like you're strong and fit enough. Come! Help this lowly criminal to His execution station!"

The Cyrene sighs in despondence until he looks down and sees Me. His eyes go wide and round with surprise and pity. No doubt he has heard stories about Me and about the miraculous things I have done. He sprints to My side, hoists the pole of My crucifix, and begins walking Me up Golgotha. Soon I can muster a miniscule amount of strength, and together we bear My cross.

Finally, we arrive at the flat, plain-like peak of Calvary's hill.

"Thank you, My friend," I pant, looking at Simon with gratitude in My eyes. "God be good to you and your family." The Cyrene seems as though he might break down and weep as he nods and turns back to reenter the crowd.

After Simon leaves, the Romans waste no time in stripping off My robes. Then, they take My tunic and even My loin-cloth, making it clear that I am not going to retain an ounce of dignity or privacy as I die. As soon as My sandals come off, I feel an elbow jab Me in the stomach and I fall backwards. I give a yelp of stunning pain as My nearly skinless back comes into contact with the rough ruggedness of the cross. Some of the wood had been sticking straight up, and it punctures My exposed veins, drawing blood even before the most gruesome torture begins.

Watching Me writhe in pain, one of the Roman guards approaches My side with a mallet and two nails. He holds one nail so that it is just grazing my wrist, which is already bloody, blue, and cold from the tightly bound cords and lack of circulation. Knowing what awaits Me now, I bite My tongue and hold My breath in an effort to somehow dull the effect of the blow.

It is useless.

"Agh!"

I give a howling, groaning shriek as an iron spike is driven into My wrist. I look over in horror as the dark red comes gushing out. It looks like a hideous, red fountain. I give another painful, gut-wrenching wail as two more spikes are pounded into My other wrist and arches of My feet with loud booms, like the thunder of My Father's wrath that had been poured out onto Me last night in the garden.

Next comes the dreadful, shrill creaking as the Romans raise Me up on My cross for all to see. As I am being lifted up, the fountains of blood issuing from My hands and feet begin to pour downward, taking the form of small, gory waterfalls, flowing onto the dirt, making pools near the foot of My cross. All the while, I am panting and clenching My teeth in grave pain. As I clench My teeth, I bite the small tip of My tongue off, and blood trickles out, flowing into the remains of My beard. The Romans had plucked most of it out as part of their brutal treatment of Me.[58]

As I lift My head, I find a sea of onlookers, including the chief priests and teachers of the law with their nasty sneers

---

[58] See Isaiah 50:6

and the Roman guards laughing and carrying on as they throw lots amongst themselves for My garments. Not one of My disciples has come back for Me. Wait ... is that ... John? Ah, John, My beloved! The one who comforted Me in the temple on Sunday; the one who leaned against Me at supper last night; the one who helped Peter access the high priest's courtyard. He has come to see Me.

I also see My mother. *Ah, Mama, I grieve for you that you must witness this! All I want to do is take you in My arms, as you had for Me many years, and shelter you from this awful sight.* Of course, My other women followers are still here as well, their faces still white, eyes still red-rimmed with mourning.

Soon, a loud uproar begins as I hear mocking voices call out,

"He could save others, but now, He cannot save Himself!"

"If this man really is the Messiah, He can just leap off that cross at any time!"

"Let God come and save Him now if He wants Him, if He is truly God's beloved Son!"

Upon hearing this, the crowd, the very same crowd who was waving branches and singing songs of praise to Me on Sunday, yell out in agreement:

"Yes, if You are the Son of God, save Yourself!"

"Ha! King of the Jews indeed!"

Even now, My heart is not ablaze with anger or wrath. Rather, it is filled with pity and sorrow for *them!* For all of them: The chief priests and teachers of the law, My betrayer Judas of Iscariot, My disowner Simon Peter, My other disciples who were not strong enough to stay by My side, even the Romans who had scourged, ridiculed, scornfully crowned, and finally nailed Me to this tree. They are *all* under the oppression of sin and Satan. I draw a deep, painful breath before wheezing out, "Father ... Forgive them ... for they know not what they do."

The people do not hear these words of love and pardon, nor do they cease their insults and scoffing. Suddenly, I hear a voice from My left side. It is a voice drowning in pain but still maintaining a jesting tone:

"Yes, Jesus ... Aren't You the Christ? Then save Yourself ... And save us, too, while You're at it!"

The voice is coming from the thief crucified on My left, who, after choking out these words, gives a deep, chesty cough.

I hang My head, but then I hear a totally different tone of voice altogether:

"Man ... don't you fear God ... even now?"

I turn My head to find that this new voice had come from the doomed convict on My right.

The thief continues, "We are under ... the same judgment ... as He is ... yet *we* deserve this punishment ... Not this man ... This man has done nothing wrong ... He is innocent."

Directing his attention to Me now, he heaves a deep, hollow sounding sigh and lays his head onto the wood of his cross. His eyes are welling with tears of sorrow, pain, guilt, and hope. "Jesus ..." he gasps shakily, "remember me ... when You come ... into Your Kingdom ..."

Oh, My son! My prodigal son! You are coming home to the Father![59]

"I tell you the truth," I answer him, My eyes and voice smiling at him even when My dry, cracked, bleeding lips cannot, "This very day ... you will be with Me ... in paradise." *I will carry him home in My arms Myself. Just as the shepherd carried his once-lost lamb joyously home and threw a celebration for its return.*

The thief on My left, upon hearing this, grunts and turns his head away, rolling his eyes. The thief on My right, however, gives another deep, shuddering sigh before closing his eyes and

---

[59] See the Parable of the Prodigal Son, found in Luke 15:11–32

breathing his last, tears streaming down his face, a peaceful half-smile on his lips.

Just then, I hear wailing. I crane My neck and see My mother, her hands covering her eyes. Despite My pain, My mind thinks back to happier times with My mother. The last memory of this kind that I can remember is this:

—◈◈◈—

Mother, the disciples, and Myself are all at a wedding in Cana. It is My first time introducing her to them. We are all talking and laughing with each other when suddenly, one of the men in charge of the wedding feast scurries out and frantically whispers something to Mother.

Mother gives a slight gasp but then relaxes a bit when she turns back to Me. Her lips form into a hopeful smile and she pulls Me aside.

"Jesus, my Son, they have no more wine. I am wondering if there is anything You could do."

"Forgive Me, My dear woman," I answer gently, "but why do you involve Me in this affair? My hour has not yet come."

I meant no disrespect by this statement. I merely meant that I did not know if My Father was ready for Me to reveal My power to My disciples yet. However, about two moments after I have spoken these words, I hear My Father speak to Me,

"Yes, My Son. It is, in fact, time. Go ahead and do what You can to make this situation right!"

My heart leaps with excitement as I nod and say, "Yes, Father! I will!"

Meanwhile, I overhear Mother whispering to the other servants, "Do whatever He tells you to do."

I smile at Mother's profound faith and motion the servants over. "You see those large ceremonial washing jars over there?" I ask them. The servants nod. "Go fill them with water." They stare at Me for a moment, confused at why I would want them to fill the jars with stale, lukewarm water when what they needed was good, fine wine. However, they do as they are told.

Once they have filled all six water jars, I say, "Good! Now draw some of the water out and take it to the master of the feast."

Nervously, the servants ladle some of the water into a cup and begin approaching the master. Unseen by them, the slightly murky water has darkened into a deep burgundy. Upon taking the cup, the master takes a small sip then proceeds to swallow the rest of the contents down, his eyes shining with mirth.

Joyously, he turns to the groom and his bride and proclaims, "Everyone brings out the choice wine first and then the cheaper wine after the guests have had too much to drink! Why have you saved the best wine 'til now?"

The bride and groom exchange bewildered looks before smiling and shrugging their shoulders, and the celebration continues. As Mother tries a sip of the wine I had made, she gives a giggle of delight and says, "Ah, Jesus, my Son, this is wonderful! Thank You! This is certainly the best wine I have ever tasted!" She now lowers her voice so as to not be heard by the nearby wedding guests and says with a wink, "You truly are Your Father's Son."

At this last comment, I chuckle heartily and pull Mother to Me, kissing her on the side of the head. "Thank you, Mother," I whisper in her ear, "for your steadfast faith and hope in Me,"

———ɷɷɷ———

Hanging here tonight, My arms outstretched, My blood is being poured out just like that wine that night, enough for all to be forgiven and redeemed. Only, this time, My mother is weeping and wringing her hands in hopelessness. *Oh, Mother, you had such great faith that night. Where is it now?*

"Woman ..." I groan in pain and pity, "behold ... your son."

Mother bites her lip and nods, her bloodshot eyes boring into My own. I can just make out the reflection of My cross and those of My fellow convicts inside her eyes; it is as if Mother is trying to take My suffering and agony upon herself.

A single tear streams down My right cheek as I muster the strength to shake My head and roll it to My side. As I do, Mother follows the line of My gaze and it leads her to John, My beloved one. He is standing completely still, frozen in shock and fear and intense grief, too much so to even cry.

"Son ..." I rasp out, "behold ... your mother."

John nods at Me, staring into My eyes. He finally breaks his gaze and finds the capacity to move towards Mother and take her into his arms, the way I would have.

It must be three in the afternoon by now. However, the once blue, cloudless skies turned dark as sackcloth three hours ago, and a cold wind is billowing out of the heavens. It reminds Me of the evening I sat by My Father's side, watching My disciples struggle on the lake. It grieved Me to see their fear and turmoil, but I waited until the time was right to go to them.

Father? Father! Where are You? Can You see Me? I have the sin of the world plastered upon My bruised, broken, bleeding body. My own mother could scarcely recognize Me through the blood! Can You see Me through the sin? Where are You? I need You, Father!

Almost the entire town is there—both My friends and My foes—eyes fixed upon My humiliating, brutal suffering. I have never felt so alone. Not during the forty days in the desert. Not after I had overthrown the disgrace in the Temple. Not after finding that My disciples could not stay awake an hour to pray with Me.

More tears cascade down My face as I cry out as hard as My failing lungs will allow Me, "Eloi, Eloi, lama sabachthani?"[60]

The Pharisees hear My lament and they shake their heads, scoffing, "What is this fool babbling about now? Is He really calling for Elijah?"

"Does He honestly think Elijah will come save His blasphemous soul?"

"Quiet, I want to see this!"

As I begin to choke and cough from increasingly difficult breath intake, My mouth and throat grow drier and drier with each gasping breath. It won't be long now.

"I am thirsty," I murmur plainly as I lay My head onto the wood.

---

[60] Aramaic for "My God, My God, why have You forsaken Me?"

One young man from out of the crowd goes and fetches a bucket of vinegar mixed with myrrh. He then sticks a sponge onto a hyssop stalk, dips it into the bucket, and raises it to My lips. *Hyssop. The very same plant used to smear the blood of the Passover lamb on the doorposts of the Hebrews' houses. Moses was right. I am the ultimate Passover Lamb in every sense of the term.*

I painfully lift My neck and take a few sips of the bitter yet refreshing drink before the Pharisees scold the man hoisting it, "Now, now, get out of the way and leave the man alone! We want to see if Elijah will indeed come down and rescue Him."

Just then, I raise My eyes and see, in the distant horizon, the back of My Father. I cannot see His face, but I can tell that He is weeping. He is weeping for Me. As He weeps, flashes of lightning crack all around Me and the whole earth trembles.

It is finished! It is finished at last! Sin and Satan are now forever vanquished! My people are free now! It is all finished! I want to throw My head back and laugh with joy and triumph. However, My lungs are growing weaker with each passing breath, and I can tell that I have very little blood left in My body. I rasp out a gurgling trio of words from My throat: "It ... is ... finished!"

I take one final breath, as the pain and the agony begin slipping from My consciousness. As I inhale, I whisper, "Father ... into Your hands ..." exhale, "I commend ... My spirit." As My exhalation trails off, I let My head drop onto My chest and everything goes black. Black as the nothingness before time. Yes, nothingness. I have nothing left now. I have lost it all. No, not *lost. Given.* I have *given* it all. I have given it all for *them.*

CHAPTER 16

"Peace be with you ... Look at My hands and My feet. It is I Myself!
Touch and see; a ghost does not have flesh and bones, as you see I have."
—Jesus (Luke 24:36, 39)

"Because you have seen Me, you have believed;
blessed are those who have not seen and yet have believed."
—Jesus to Thomas (John 20:29)

———◦◦◦———

"Jesus, My Boy! My beloved Boy! Arise! It's time to wake up!"**

I yawn and begin slowly opening My eyes before bursting them open in great excitement. *I'm alive!* Even though I already knew that I would rise, I am still in awe of this phenomenon.

The first thing I notice is that it is very cold and I am lying in a very hard bed. However, the cloth I am dressed in, including the cloth wrapped around My face, is soft. *Fine linen!* I close My eyes again and breathe in the gorgeous scent of myrrh. *Seventy-five pounds of myrrh!*

Finally, I tear the linen from My head to find Myself lying in a tomb, wrapped in fine burial clothes.

"Welcome back, Jesus, My Son! My brave, faithful, victorious Son!"

I slowly lift and turn My head to locate the source of the voice, though I already know whom I will find.

"Father! Oh, My Father!" I cry out, "You have returned to Me!" I leap from My stone shelf into My Father's open arms. "Yes, My Son! Here I am!"

"Say, Father ... You've called Me by My earthly name."

"Of course I have, My Son! Your name, Jesus, is much more than an earthly name. It is now the name above *all* names! By Your name, by calling on Your great and precious name, humankind can now have access to Me!"

My Father continues, "Jesus, My Son, You did not see this while on that cross the other night; You had already died. But the moment You took that final breath, there was so much wind and lightning that the curtain in the Holy of Holies in the Temple was torn from top to bottom! Do You know what caused that?"

After thinking a moment, I blurt out, "Was it ... Me?"

"Yes! Yes, My dear Boy," My Father gives His great, booming belly laugh, clapping Me on the back. "It was Your final breath that did away with the curtain, the barrier between humankind and Myself. Nothing can separate them from Me now!"

My eyes and mouth simultaneously go wide before I utter, "Oh, Father! I've done it! *We've* done it!"

My Father nods His head and continues to laugh with joy. He tugs now at the sleeve of My grave clothes. "Now, let's take these wrappings off of You and leave this place of the dead!"

"Gladly, Father! Gladly!"

With a clap of His hands, My Father summons two angels, one bearing a shining, white robe much like the one My robe turned into during My transfiguration, and the other holding a fresh pair of sandals. I quickly undress, noticing that My body feels so much better and stronger than it has in days, even weeks. Looking over My shoulders, I see that the skin on My back has been miraculously regenerated. Not a stripe is left from My scourging. As I toss My linen sheet aside, however, I see big, gaping, hole-shaped scars in My wrists and feet, reminders of the horrors of Friday night. There is even a scar in My side, though it is a bit finer than the four scars in My hands and feet. Of course, none of My bones were broken, as I was already dead when the Romans examined My body. *The prophecy![61]*

"Yes, My Son," My Father answers, "I have left those scars in Your hands, feet, and side so that when You appear to Your

---

[61] See John 19:36–37

disciples, they may see and believe that You are really, physically risen and not a ghost or vision!"

By now, I am fully dressed and ready to get out of this tomb. As I am about to exit, however, My Father wags His finger and says, "Wait a minute, Son. Aren't You going to fold up Your napkins first?"

"Fold up My napkins?" I ask in confusion. Then I look down and see My burial clothes wadded in a heap on the stone shelf. I blush and abashedly look back at My Father.

"You see, Jesus, My Son, when a master is eating, a servant will watch to see what he does with his napkin. If he lays it down unfolded, it tells the servant, 'I am finished; you may clear my dishes now.' But if he folds up his napkin, it means, 'Do not clear my dishes yet; I am coming back.'[62] And You have! Fold up those napkins!"

"Yes, Father! I shall fold them up right away!"

I neatly fold up My burial clothes and the cloth that had been wrapped around My head and set them onto the shelf, with the sheet at the foot and the facial napkin at the head.

---

[62] Biven, N. David. "Christ's Linen Napkin (John 20:7): Is It Significant That the Napkin That Had Been Around Jesus' Head When He Was Buried Was Found In The Empty Tomb Folded?" *Jerusalem Perspective*. 7 October 2006. Web. 19 April 2018

"Excellent!" My Father exclaims. "Now, let's get You out of here!"

With another clap of His hands, another mighty angel comes down from Heaven and, with a wondrous shaking of the ground, rolls the huge, round stone from the door of the tomb. I saunter out the door, into the sunlight, and find that the whole garden is gloriously in bloom. The trees are swaying their branches as though dancing in joy and praise, and the birds are chirping and singing even more sweetly than usual. After warming Myself in the sun for a few moments, I stroll under the shade of one of the trees, and it rains down its blossoms upon My head, creating a much richer, softer, more fragrant crown than the one I wore two nights ago. It seems as though the whole of creation is singing and dancing with joy upon My resurrection.

Suddenly, My eyes behold a sight that both alarms and amuses Me at the same time: Two Roman guards lying facedown on the grass outside My tomb! They look like they are dead!

"Fear not, My Son. They will be all right," My Father says with a chuckle. "As soon as they wake up, they will go to their masters with the insane lie that Your disciples came and stole Your body away during the night. In doing so, many people will be disillusioned for years to come."

"What? Are You serious?!" I exclaim in incredulousness before throwing My head back in a peal of laughter and rolling My eyes. "Ha! Foolish men! Foolish, foolish men!"

"Yes, My Son, but don't worry. Your disciples will know better. So will many others after them."

After speaking these words, My Father leads Me to the door of My tomb and reveals a patch of large, delicate, white, trumpet-shaped flowers. *Lilies?*

"Now, these flowers, Son. They make You sneeze, yes?"

I nod inquisitively.

"Not anymore! This is Your new, resurrected body! It is perfect and infallible now! Nothing can hurt You again! Not death, not sickness, not physical pain, not even the powerful aroma of these white lilies. Go ahead, try them!"

Eagerly, I take one of the flowers from My Father's hand and hold it to My nose, breathing in its sweet perfume. Sure enough, I find that I am not sneezing, and My eyes are not tearing up. The fragrance of the lily is sweet but light. It is pleasant to My senses, not overwhelming to them.

"Ah, Father, this is wonderful! Thank You very much!"

"Of course, My Son. It is My desire for all My children to be able to enjoy My creation completely freely, without restriction."

"Very good, Father! Oh, but back to My resurrected body—"

"Oh, yes, My Son. I have also created You to be able to travel wherever You want to instantly, even through locked doors. You can never hunger or thirst again while on earth, nor can You ever feel excessive exhaustion. This means that You never need to worry about eating, drinking, or sleeping, although You will certainly be *able* to do these activities and take pleasure in them. As I have stated before, You can never die or be physically hurt again for the remainder of Your stay in this world. Where is death's sting now? Where is the grave's victory now? *And,* through *Your* resurrection, humankind may now receive new, resurrected bodies and eternal life with Us!"

Again, I am at a loss for words as I listen to My Father go on in His joy and exhilaration. The immense joy I am now feeling far surpasses any pain I had experienced during My death. Finally, He finishes and takes Me in His arms as He whispers, "Soon, My Son, You will be coming home with Me, where We will never be separated from one another again!"

"Home, My Father?"

I have never had a definite home while here on earth; even when I was born, My parents and I were on the road, and we had to run from the government that wanted to kill Me.[63] Even

the foxes have their dens and the birds their nests, but I had

nowhere.[64] Just the reminder of having a home waiting for Me

at all, let alone in My Father's love, where I will never be sepa-

rated from Him again, brings tears of joy to My eyes.

"Yes, Jesus, My Son! Home at My right hand! After all, You

have many mansions to build up there." He adds this last remark

with a wink.

"Quite right, Father," I reply with a smile.

Just then, I hear frantic footsteps and a woman's desperate,

sobbing voice calls out, "Sir … ? Sir? A-, are You the gardener?"

Perhaps she sees the lily I still grasp in My hand.

"Ah, My Son, You have a visitor! Mary of Magdalene. Go, com-

fort her and reveal Yourself to her!"

"Yes, Father!"

I pull from My Father's embrace and begin approaching

Mary. "Woman, woman, why are you crying? Who is it that you

are seeking?"

"Oh, Sir …" Mary pants, the skin around her eyes bruise-col-

ored from excessive weeping, "If You are … the one who took

---

[63] See Matthew 2:13–15

[64] See Matthew 8:20

our Lord Jesus from His tomb ... please tell me where You have placed Him ... so that I may get Him." The very speaking of My name causes Mary's heart to break anew. After giving this plea, she buries her face into her hands and continues to sob.

When I see this, My heart melts and I utter one single, tender word: "Mary." By now, I am standing right in front of Mary. I take her face into My hands and gently dry her tears with My thumbs. Once her vision is cleared, she looks and sees the scars in the hands cupping her cheeks and the eyes staring lovingly into her own.

"Rabbi? *My* Rabbi? My Rabbi Jesus? Can it be?!" she gasps in shock and great joy. She begins trembling and quickly throws her arms around Me, resting her head upon My chest, both out of affection and for support.

For a few moments, I just stand there, patting and rubbing circles on her back to calm her. All the while, I whisper in her ear, "Ah, Mary ... My sweet Mary ... Do not be afraid ... I am here ... Everything is all right now."

Eventually, I feel a tap on My shoulder; It is My Father. He smiles warmly and motions Me over. I nod, clear My throat to get Mary's attention, and speak earnestly yet gladly, "Mary, do not cling to Me right now, for I have yet to return to My

Father. But right now, I need you to go and tell My disciples, My brothers, that I am alive and will soon be going back to My Father, who is now your Father, My God, who is now your God!"

I kiss Mary tenderly on the forehead and send her off, but not before looking back into her eyes and murmuring, "Mary ... tell Peter."

———oɷo———

I happily watch Mary skip off, her feet barely touching the ground as she sings out at the top of her voice, "I have seen Him! I have seen the Lord! He is alive!"

My Father then takes Me by the shoulder, His eyes shining with mirth, and says, "Now, My Son, let Us go onto the road to Emmaus. There are some friends of Yours in need of Your comfort."

In a flash, there We are. My Father flips My cowl upon My head.

"My Son, do not reveal Your identity until I tell You it is time."

"All right, Father," I answer, noting the sly grin forming on My Father's lips.

The two men are just ten paces up the road from Us. I recognize one of them as Cleopas, a man not in My circle of twelve, but still a true and faithful disciple. Walking a little closer, I realize that the second man is none other than Joseph of Arimathea,[65] the very same man who helped Nicodemus carry out My burial plan. *Won't he be surprised to see Me!*

"Hello there, gentlemen," I call out. "Do you mind if I join you two?"

The men turn to face Me. When they do, I see tear stains on their cheeks and their eyes are bloodshot, with shadows underneath them. I detect hollowness and congestion in their voices as they reply, "Er ... all right. Are You trying to escape Jerusalem as well?"

I can tell that they have been crying, perhaps for the past two days. Though I am aware of the reason, I feign a surprised tone as I inquire, "Why, no! Whatever are you escaping from? What has happened that you look so glum this fine morning?"

The men exchange sad and incredulous glances before turning back to Me, eyes filling anew with tears.

"Ah, Sir. You must be the only one in town who has not heard of the terrible event that took place the other day," Cleopas moans, shaking his head sadly.

"What terrible event?"

---

[65] Creative license: The identity of the second disciple on the road to Emmaus is unknown.

"Why, the crucifixion of our Lord Jesus of Nazareth, of course!" Joseph exclaims, a hint of bitterness in his voice.

"Hmmm," I purr as I rub the bristles of My newly restored beard, all the while itching to reveal Myself to the men right here and now.

Cleopas chimes back in, "We truly believed that He was the great prophet; the one who would save our people, Israel."

"Well, of course! The Messiah!" I answer.

"The Messiah?" Joseph asks, frowning with puzzlement. "But how could that be? How could the Messiah be put to death like a common criminal?"

I chuckle and shake My head. "Oh, foolish men!" I rebuke. "Do you not remember your ancient prophecies? The Messiah *needed* to die in order to be glorified! Come, we shall explore these prophecies together."

And we do. Beginning with the Passover lamb in the second scroll of Moses, on through Isaiah and Micah, I show them all to My disciples.

"Surely, He has borne our griefs
   and carried our sorrows;
   yet we esteemed Him stricken,
   smitten by God, and afflicted.

But He was wounded for our transgressions,

He was bruised for our iniquities.

The chastisement for our peace was upon Him,

And by His stripes, we are healed.

All we, like sheep, have gone astray;

We have turned, every one, to his own way;

And the Lord has laid on Him the iniquity of us all."[66]

———

By now, we have reached Emmaus and have checked into an inn.

"Er, well, Sir, You certainly know Your prophecies," Cleopas replies, sounding somewhat cheerier than before, "but what exactly does this mean for us now?"

"It is time, My Son," My Father whispers, placing a hand on My shoulder. "Reveal Yourself!"

I smile and look deeply into My disciples' eyes.

"Wait ... who *are* You?" Joseph breathes in wonder.

"Must you ask, My friend?" I ask in a voice barely above a whisper.

Suddenly, Cleopas begins sniffing the air. "Say, Joseph," he says, "do you smell something?"

---

[66] Isaiah 53:4–6

Joseph takes a whiff and slowly breaks into a smile. "Ahh, yes, I do, my friend. It smells like ... myrrh? Am I going insane, or is the fragrance coming from—?" He turns to Me.

"Yes, Joseph," I answer, brushing the cowl from My head. "It is. Courtesy of you and our friend, Nicodemus!"

My smile broadens as I roll up the sleeves of My robe, revealing the nail marks. My two friends go white and look as though they might faint as a bright light envelops Me and, in the blink of an eye, I leave them.

———

Next, I find Myself outside the door of the upper room where I had shared My last supper with My disciples. The door is barred up; however, I can still hear the disconsolate voices within:

"I still can't believe Jesus is dead! What are we going to do without Him?"

"What if they come for *us?*"

"Are we just supposed to stay in here forever?"

"And to think that the last time I spoke to Him, I called Him a lunatic."[67]

---

[67] See Mark 3:21

This last phrase was spoken by My mother, and after saying this, she breaks down and sobs.

"Old Simeon was right! A sword *has* indeed pierced through my soul!"[68]

Finally, I can bear it no longer. With a side step, I leap right through the wall and land perfectly in the middle of the room.

"Shalom,[69] peace be with you, My friends! Here I am!" I cry out. Upon hearing My voice, everyone is so shocked that they stop crying and slowly turn to face the source of the voice they had just heard.

For several moments, the whole room is absolutely silent. Suddenly, Philip screams, "Eek! Now He really *is* a Ghost!"

I laugh, roll up My sleeves, and say, "No, no, no! I am *not* a ghost! Look here! Look at My hands! Look at My feet! Look at My side! Touch them, if you would like. See the dried blood on the scars? A ghost does not have flesh and blood and bone, does it?"

I turn and approach Mother. She is shaking all over, from both shock and great joy, much like Mary had this morning.

"Jesus ... my Son? You're ... alive?" she whispers.

---

[68] See Luke 2:32b

[69] Hebrew word meaning, "Peace"

She takes My hands into her own, gasping in horror and pity, "Are ... are those Your ... hands?!"

"Yes, Mama," I croon as I take her into My arms and kiss her on the forehead. "Oh, Mama, please do not be angry with yourself. I know, I might have seemed to have lost My mind back then, and even recently. It was the crazy, reckless, extravagant love I had for you, for everyone in this room, and for the whole world that led Me to give Myself up to the powers of sin and death. Through My death and now resurrection, sin's curse is removed, and death's sting is no more!"

"Oh, My Son," Mother murmurs, resting her head on My chest, listening to the sound of My beating heart. "Now I see that You are much more than my Son: You are my Savior! The Savior of us all!"

Hearing Mother's and My words, everyone comes and gathers around Me, bowing low in true reverence. Together we laugh and weep with great joy and gladness. Soon, though, I collect Myself, clear My throat, and breathe on them.

"This is the breath of the Holy Spirit. Welcome Him into your hearts and lives. The Spirit is the one who has helped Me to do the wondrous miracles I have done. However, now you shall do these same works *and greater.* He will also give you the power to give and withhold forgiveness from anyone who asks. Now, let's eat! You folks need your strength."

At My words, everyone breaks into a smile, gathers around the table with Me, and together, we eat, drink, and laugh, basking in each other's company just like we did before.

—⁓—

The next week, I again appear outside the door of the upper room. This time, I hear, happy, joyful voices:

"We are telling you He is alive!"

"We have seen Him with our own eyes!"

"Come on, Thomas! Do you honestly think I wouldn't know my own Son?"

Thomas? Thomas! Of course! Thomas was the only one of My true disciples who had not been present when I appeared to everyone last week. He skipped town to wait until the buzz centered on My death had desisted. He has just returned.

Next, I hear the sad, hollow voice of My doubting disciple sigh, "Please, my friends, don't raise my hopes. I love and miss Jesus just as much as you people do. But how can I be sure that you actually saw Him, and that your grief and lack of sleep haven't caused you to see things? Listen, unless I myself see Him and can touch and feel the scars in His hands and side, I will not believe!"

Hearing these brokenhearted words, I creep through the wall and touch Thomas' neck tenderly. "Ah, Thomas," I purr, "peace be with you."

Slowly, Thomas turns and finds himself staring into the absolute compassion and grace of My eyes. His mouth nearly falls to the floor as he tries to speak, but the words won't come.

"Thomas, My friend, come! Put your finger in My hand. Put your hand in My side. Experience My resurrection and My life. Let go of your doubts and just believe!"

Finally, Thomas sinks down at My pierced feet and chokes out, "My Lord … and my God!"

"Yes, Thomas," I whisper back. "You believe because you have seen Me. You have experienced Me firsthand. Blessed are those who have not seen Me but yet believe."

"Oh, Jesus! Jesus!" Thomas sobs. "Please forgive my lack of faith! I've missed You so much."

I get down on the ground and hold the man in My arms, rubbing his back and shoulders. After he has calmed down enough, I breathe on him and explain to him everything that he had missed while on the run last week: How it was his sin and My love for him that I died for and how it was because of him that I did not stay dead; how it was My love for every individual person on earth that rendered the powers of sin and death powerless.

Ah, but there is one more disciple that I must reach out to especially. This disciple *appeared* to be just as glad and excited about My return as the others, if not more so. But when it came to actually sitting and eating with Me, everything inside of him seemed to change, and he became aloof and distant toward Me. I, of course, know why, and it breaks My heart. My desire is to tear down every barrier separating Me from the ones I love.

Simon Peter, My disowner, is no exception.

CHAPTER 17

"Simon, son of Jonah, do you love Me?"
"Lord, You know all things; You know that I love You."
"Feed My sheep."
Jesus and Peter (John 21:17)

"And surely, I am with you always, even to the end of the age!"
Jesus (Matthew 28:20)

———※———

S ome days later, at Peter's suggestion, the eleven go out fishing. *What? Fishing? For **fish**? I called them to be fishers of **men**! Don't they understand that My mission for them is not finished? It is just beginning!*

I appear on the beach of Galilee. I cup My hands around My mouth and yell out, "My boys, have you caught anything this morning?"

Peter calls back, "No, Sir! We haven't caught a single fish all *night!*"

I give a mischievous grin. "Throw your net over the other side of your boat! See what you catch!" *For old time's sake!*

Peter gives the sons of Zebedee a puzzled look. No doubt they had switched sides many times throughout the night. Eventually, however, the men shrug their shoulders and throw their nets. As I expected, two moments later, they lurch forward. The nets do not get full to the point of breaking as they did the day we first met, but the eleven are still amazed.

Suddenly, John's eyes go wide as he takes Peter's shoulder, motions to Me on the beach, and says, "Say, Peter? Haven't we seen this before? Do you suppose that fellow on the beach is—"

"It's the Lord! It's Jesus! He's really back!"

Peter takes a breath and dives headfirst into the lake. Off he swims to meet Me on shore, with the rest of My disciples rowing fast behind him.

———∞∞∞———

I am warming up some bread to go with the fish the trio has caught when Peter comes up, panting and dripping wet. I rise to embrace him.

"Ah, good to see you, Peter! Come, breakfast is served!"

During breakfast, I look up from My piece of fish and touch Peter's arm. "Simon Peter, son of Jonah, do you love Me more than the others?"

Peter smiles warmly at Me and says, "Yes, Lord, You know I love You."

I smile back at him and say, "Feed My lambs."

We resume our eating. A couple minutes later, I look at Peter and ask a second time, "Simon Peter, son of Jonah, do you love Me?"

Peter stares at Me in confusion before answering, "Er, yes Lord! You know I love you!"

"Tend My sheep," I reply, My smile growing larger.

After another two minutes, I ask yet again, "Simon Peter, son of Jonah, do you *truly* love Me?"

Peter's shoulders slump as he makes the connection: I am asking him to declare his love to Me for every time that he denied Me on Friday morning. He closes his eyes and tears cascade down his cheeks.

"Lord. Jesus," he answers thickly, "You know all things. You know that I love You."

My smile softens as I take pity on My disciple's distress. I take him in My arms and whisper in his ear, "Feed My sheep."

I now push Peter up by his chest so that we are at eye level. "Peter," I say earnestly, "when you were younger, you were free to dress yourself and go wherever you wished. However, when you grow older, your hands will be stretched out and others will dress you and take you where you do not wish to go."

"Just like what they did to You," Peter gasps in wonder after thinking over My words.

Then, he turns toward John, sitting by his brother, James. He turns back to Me and asks, "Lord, what about that man? What about our friend, John? What will happen to *him?* What will *he* do?"

After setting My eyes upon John, I chuckle and shake My head. "Peter, do not worry about John. Whether I want him to live until My return or not, that is none of your concern. Your concern is to follow Me. Follow Me in your own way."

———

By now, it has been forty days since My resurrection, and I am ready to go home to My Father. I lead My disciples, now apostles,[70] up the Mount of Olives. Once there, I give them final words of instruction:

---

[70] Though sometimes used interchangeably, the terms *disciple* and *apostle* are slightly different. A *disciple* is someone who learns from one specific person; a student. An apostle is anyone who has had an encounter with the risen Christ.

"My friends, do not leave Jerusalem until you have received the promised Holy Spirit. My cousin, John the Baptist, baptized you with water, but I shall soon baptize you with the Holy Spirit."

Peter, excited by My words, says, "Wait, Lord! Since You are leaving soon, does that mean You are now going to restore the throne of David to Israel?" The rest of the assembly starts murmuring in eager anticipation.

"Peace, My friends," I state firmly. "It is not for you to know when these things will happen. Only the Father has the authority to know. Rather, you *yourselves* shall receive power when the Holy Spirit comes upon you. And you shall be My witnesses in Jerusalem and in all Judea, and Samaria, and to all the ends of the earth. Go, therefore, and make disciples of *all* nations, baptizing them in the name of the Father and of the Son and of the Holy Spirit, and teaching them to obey everything I have commanded you."

As I am speaking, a cloud comes down from heaven to cover Me. I know that it is from My Father. It is time. He is ushering Me home. Rising on the cloud, I shout a final reminder to My friends, "And surely, I am with you always, even to the end of the age!"

Finally, the clouds cover up the forms of My apostles and I can see them no longer. In the blink of an eye, I find Myself in a grand throne room. *My Father's throne room!* When My Father sees Me, He comes racing towards Me, arms wide open.

"Welcome home, Jesus, My Son!" He cries. He grabs Me and takes Me in His arms in a nearly bone-crushing hug and begins kissing Me. "Come, enter into Your throne and Kingdom!"

My Father waves His hand in front of Me to reveal a marvelous, white throne positioned to the right of His own throne. "Come! Sit!" He invites.

Eagerly, I do as I am asked and sit on My glorious throne. *Ah! Home at last!*

—⌘—

My Father and I have all the time in the world—well, in eternity—to talk, and I love thinking and brainstorming with Him about the mansions I'll be preparing for My apostles. "Father?" I ask. "Would You mind if I get a head start on the mansions? I have a lot of ideas."

"No, not at all," My Father answers tenderly. "The Kingdom is Yours now. You have all eternity to work on those mansions. You also have the important job of mediating on behalf of repentant sinners when they come to Me. Remember, there is no time in this place as there is on earth. Now, go! Attend to those mansions!" Then, with a twinkle in His eye, My Father adds, "And have fun, My Son. You bring Me great joy!"

CHAPTER 18

"This man (Saul) is My chosen instrument to proclaim My name to the Gentiles and their kings and to the people of Israel."
—*Jesus to Ananias (Acts 9:15)*

"Behold, I am coming soon! My reward is with Me, and I will give to each person according to what they have done."
—*Jesus to John the Beloved (Revelation 22:7)*

———❧———

T rue to My word, I get right to work, furnishing the mansions for each and every one of My apostles. All the while, I am looking down upon them and smiling at what they are doing. I watch as the Holy Spirit first appears unto them, their heads all aglow with His flame, and listen as they shout and call out My praise in all the tongues of the nations. I sing over them with joy and love as they begin forming My church, under Peter's leadership, of course. Many people come and listen and choose to follow Me. They break bread and pour wine together in memory of Me, sing songs of worship together, and are baptized and in turn baptize others. There is great excitement and celebration in My Kingdom.

Soon, however, I return to My Father's right hand to begin ushering and welcoming My friends home. The first friend to arrive is a young man named Stephen. Stephen was one of My converted followers who had listened to Peter's preaching. He had angered the Pharisees by proclaiming My name to them. While he was preaching to them, his face shining as brightly as an angel's, the Pharisees grew so angry that they dragged him out into the street and began stoning him.

As soon as I saw this, I rose from My throne at My Father's right hand, stooped down, and held out My own hand for Stephen to take when the time came. The last words I heard him speak before taking My hand and breathing his last were,

"Lord ... receive my spirit ... But hold not ... these men's sin ... against them!"

Once Stephen is safe in My arms, I embrace him and murmur, "My precious, precious Stephen, of course I won't. In fact, one of these men I will even use to bring more people to My glory as you have done!"

The man in question is not one who took part in Stephen's stoning, but a young Pharisee in charge of holding the others' cloaks while they did the stoning and who congratulated them after the sordid ordeal. His name is Saul.

———❧———

Poor Saul! He has been blinded by the devil and the other Pharisees into believing the lie that I was still dead and that by worshiping Me, My apostles were blaspheming My Father. I must go and heal him of this blindness so that he may truly see Me as I am and help others to see the same.

One day, Saul is called to go into Damascus. His mission is to capture some of My followers and slay others. He had already arrested My friends Peter and James, the brother of John. James was even beheaded by Herod Agrippa. However, Peter escaped prison by means of an angelic rescue.

While watching Saul on his way down the road to wreak his havoc, I blaze My light in his path, startling his horse and knocking him onto the walkway.

"Saul! Saul!" I rebuke with tears in My eyes. "Why are you persecuting Me?"

Shielding his eyes as best as he can, the awestruck man stammers out, "Who *are* You … Lord?"

"I am Jesus," I answer. "I am alive, and when you hurt My followers, you are hurting Me as well. Now go into the city. Someone there will give you further instruction."

As I leave Saul and return to My Father's side, I turn back and watch as Saul gropes around, crying out for assistance, his eyes stripped of their color. He is now physically blind. Only in being so shall he truly see.

Next, I appear to one of My followers in Damascus, Ananias. I tell him to go into the village and pray over My soon to be apostle that he might receive not only his physical sight, but also his spiritual sight, the Holy Spirit. At first, Ananias balks at this command. "Lord, do You mean Saul of Tarsus? The man who has done terrible things to Your people in Jerusalem?"

I just smile and answer, "Yes, that is indeed the man I speak of. You see, I have called him to a special mission: He shall speak My word to the Gentiles[71] and their kings and to the people of Israel. Now, go!"

My servant stands in awe for a moment before rising and leaving to attend to Saul.

—⟊⟊⟊—

Once Saul, now changed to *Paul,* is healed and baptized, I watch with utmost gladness as he gains the trust of the other apostles, learns more about Me by listening to their preaching, and begins his mission. I watch over him, protect him throughout

[71] Non-Jewish population

his travels, and comfort him during his persecutions, imprison-ments, and shipwrecks. I give him the power to speak My word with authority before his accusers and even the power to heal. Like Myself, even the very touch of his garments is enough to make the sick whole.[72]

Eventually, I stoop down again and reach out My hand as I see Paul approaching his Roman executioner. The mighty *thwack!* of the executioner's axe is drowned out by My apostle's joyous proclamation of "Jesus! Master! I have come home to You!"

"Ahh, yes! Welcome home, My friend! My faithful servant, Paul," I answer, hugging him tightly. "Come, let Me show you to your mansion!"

By now, nearly all of My original, true disciples are forever safe and sound in My Father's house: James, as already stated, beheaded by Herod Agrippa; Thomas, driven through with a spear; Matthew, stabbed in the back with Hertecus' sword; the other James stoned, beaten, and finally killed by a club to the head; and Peter, Andrew, Philip, Thaddeus, Simon the Zealot,

---

[72] See Acts 19:12

and Matthias, the apostle chosen to replace Judas,[73] flogged and crucified. Andrew was tied rather than nailed to prolong his suffering, while his brother hung upside-down (he claimed he was unworthy of dying in the exact same fashion as I did).[74]

However, there is one sole surviving disciple who has yet to make it Home.

———❧———

With a mighty flash of lightning, I appear to John, My beloved disciple, who had been exiled to the island of Patmos. With Me are seven golden lampstands, and in My hand are seven stars, representing the seven churches in Asia Minor and their angels. I am dressed in a long, white robe with a golden sash around My waist; My hair is white as wool, My eyes like burning fires.

Upon seeing Me, John falls down at My feet as though dead. I smile tenderly, place My right hand on him, and declare in a voice like a thousand waterfalls, "Fear not, John. I am the Alpha and the Omega, the Beginning and the End, the Almighty One

---

[73] Judas committed suicide after failing to bail Jesus out. However, his actual cause of death is a subject of debate. Matthew's account tells of him simply hanging himself (27:3–10), whereas Luke the physician, in the book of Acts, goes into more gruesome detail about him throwing himself off a cliff, his stomach exploding mid-fall (1:18). Matthias was the man chosen to replace Judas as an apostle (Acts 1:23).

[74] Kiger, Patrick J. "How Did the Apostles Die?" *National Geographic*. 19 February 2015. Web. 10 April 2018

and the Living One, the One who was dead but is now alive forever!" John opens his eyes and sees My feet, which are now blazing like refined, polished bronze. There, at their arches, are two nail scars.

John gives a gasp at this sight and whispers, "Lord? Jesus? Is it really You?"

"Yes, John, here I am. Now, write a letter to the seven churches and tell them what you have just seen, what is happening now, and what is yet to be."

As soon as John has grabbed a scroll, pen, and ink, I have him write down to the seven churches My applauses, My rebukes, My instructions, and My promises to them. I then proceed to show him a wondrous vision of the future. As I do, I change forms.

First I become a Lamb that had been slain but was yet alive, and I open the seven seals of My Father's judgment upon the earth. Next, I turn into a tiny Baby in a woman's arms, pursued by Satan, the ancient serpent and deceiver of the nations, and I am caught up into heaven, returned to My adult form, and given a scepter with which to rule. After this, I am a mighty Angel with a rainbow over My head and a sickle in My hand, harvesting the grapes to put into the winepress of My Father's wrath. Finally, I revert back to My first appearance and triumph over Satan, his false prophet, and their servants, once and for all, striking them down with the double-edged sword coming out from My mouth. Once the battle is won, I ride on a magnificent white horse as the true Word of God on My way to meet My bride, the new Jerusalem. The *true* Jerusalem. The holy city made up of every one of My true followers, apostles, and friends.

There, I show John around the city: the gates of pearl, engraved with the names of the tribes of Israel; the foundation stones with the names of My apostles, including John's own name; the streets of purest gold; the tree of life watered by the river of life flowing from My throne.

"There will be no more pain or crying or death or night here, for the old order of things will have passed away," I promise John. "Tell the churches that I am coming soon and great is My reward for everyone who overcomes!"

"Amen!" John exclaims, his eyes shining with tears of joy. "Come, Lord Jesus!"

—⦿—

Five years after My appearance to John on Patmos, at long last, I come to the island once again. I look through the window of John's hut and see John asleep, curled up on his side, a small, feeble, yet peaceful smile on his face. As he is sleeping, his face goes ashen and he gives a deep, ghastly exhalation.[75]

As soon as I hear this sound, I enter the hut, cradle My beloved disciple in My arms, and ascend back Home. Once back at My Father's right hand, I say, "John, My beloved friend! Wake up! We are home!"

John's eyes slowly begin to flutter before bursting open upon realizing where he is and who is holding him. "Jesus! Lord! Friend!" he cries, "I'm home! I'm really home! With You! With the others!"

At the sound of John's voice, the other apostles—Peter, Andrew, John's brother James, Philip, Nathanael, Thomas, Matthew, the other James, Thaddeus, Simon, Matthias, Stephen, Paul, and a host of others—sprint out of My Father's house, gather around him and hug and kiss him. Together, we sit down at the banquet table of My Father and eat and drink and laugh and celebrate, just like old times. Just like it was always meant to be.

---

[75] John the Beloved was the only one of the original twelve disciples to die a natural, peaceful death.

—∽∾∽—

My dear reader,

The events recorded in the book you have just read are true. I did leave My Father's right hand and come dwell among human-kind. I did not want the glories of Heaven if it meant your eternal separation from My Father and Me, so I brought Heaven down to you. I was born and lived a perfect, sinless life. I did perform many miracles; more miracles than the writer of this book had room to mention; even more than the original gospel writers had room to mention; miracles of power but more than that, miracles of love and compassion.

When My earthly work was done, I did suffer horrendous, unimaginable pain, torment, and death on a rugged Roman cross. As I was dying, I was thinking about you and My vast, unfathom-able love for you. While you were still a sinner, while you still did not regard Me, I suffered it all for you. I died for you personally. Even if you were the only sinner on earth, I still would have died to sanctify you of your sin. But I also did not stay dead; I rose

220

to life again for you, giving you the power to also rise and live again in Me.

After you close this book and set it down, I want you to be like My friend Thomas and worship Me as your Lord and your God. I want you to be like My friend Simon Peter and proclaim your love for Me and commit your life to following Me in your own special, wonderful way. I want you to be like My friends Stephen and Paul, ready and willing to tell others about Me, even if it costs you everything you have, even your very life. Finally, I want you to be like My friend John, faithful to the end and open to receive whatever signs and revelations I choose to share with you.

As I first told John on the Island of Patmos, I am coming soon, and great is My reward to you who overcome. Dearly beloved, won't you choose to be a part of My new, true, beautiful Jerusalem today?

Your spotless Lamb, your risen Lord, your Friend who sticks closer than a brother, and your coming Bridegroom King,

Jesus Christ

CPSIA information can be obtained
at www.ICGtesting.com
Printed in the USA
BVHW061653080419
544915BV00017B/1556/P

9 781545 652886